The Single Twin

David Reynolds-Moreton

sci-fi-cafe.com

One:
Lone Voyager

THE WARNING SCREAM of the tug's 'something up ahead' system brought Cresswell back to present time with a jolt.

He hit the cancel button with far more force than was necessary, as the alarm set his nerves on edge with its persistent screeching, like a piece of sharp steel on glass.

Swinging round from the course programming controls, he gazed intently into the forward viewing screen to see what had triggered the alarm system. At first there was nothing to see, except for the star field spread out before him like a black velvet drape spangled with diamonds.

When the alarm sounder was off, the warning light was still flashing, so something must be out there. And then he saw it, a large dark spinning object, blanking out the stars.

Fortunately his instruments showed he wasn't on a collision course with the object, but would pass it by at a distance of about half a kilometre or so as the tug accelerated on its outward journey. As he drew nearer to the large black cylinder, the letters KC17 were plainly visible on its side.

Opening up the communication unit, he called in to the smelter station to report his find, as space debris was a constant hazard this close to earth. He gave the cylinder's position and code number, and then sat back patiently for the reply.

Suddenly the radiation monitor began bleeping, so he turned the remote scanning head in the direction of the mysterious cylinder, and the beep rate went up nearly off the scale. Cresswell then guessed what the cylinder was, and a flush of anger went through him.

He turned back to the main controls and switched off the automatics, turning the little tug off to one side so that it would safely distance itself from the radiation source.

At that moment the speaker over his head crackled into life and he was informed it was 'Only another load of nuclear waste being sent on its way' by a disinterested voice with a suitably monotonous tone to add to the lack of interest and complete disregard for the consequences.

'The irresponsible sods.' he muttered to himself as he reset the auto pilot. It had been common practice for quite a long time to dispose of nuclear waste in this manner, and it wasn't until one of the cylinders had fallen back to earth burning up in a blazing fire ball and trailing a cloud of radioactive particles behind it, that the peoples of earth spoke with one voice. All three governments promised faithfully never to use this method of disposal again, but of course they did; only the public didn't know about it.

The shuttles which took the refined minerals down to earth, came back up again virtually empty. Some bright spark realized that it would cost very little extra to take the waste up in them, and then with a suitable propulsion unit and control system attached, sent on an inward spiral towards the sun to be consumed harmlessly upon arrival. Some even brighter spark then realized that a few credits more could be saved if the cylinders were just jettisoned from the shuttles as they approached the smelters, the momentum carrying them on, and hopefully out of the solar system.

The fact that space was going to be littered with a large number of cylinders chock full of man's unwanted radioactive waste didn't seem to bother anyone, least of all the governments of the three nations.

He had heard rumours of the scheme, but always dismissed them as being too stupid. This was the first time he had witnessed the results of the disposal process, and felt an even deeper mistrust and disgust for his fellow man.

Cresswell Ã–rgsveltd, because of his dislike and distrust for mankind in general, would liked to have lived on a remote desert island, as far away from his fellow man as was humanly possible. But as such islands were as scarce as hen's teeth, and the yearly rental for one would have taken at least three lifetimes of his savings, he gave up on the idea, and settled for the next best thing.

He became a Rock Jockey, or to give it a more correct and scientific name, the Captain, Chief Engineer, Pilot, Navigator, Chef, Head Bottle Washer and General Factotum on a small, one-man, but very powerful, space tug, whose sole purpose was to go out to the asteroid belt, locate suitably sized chunks of metal ore, or if one was very lucky, a piece of pure metal, and bring them back to one of the smelting stations which encircled Earth.

The so called Great Nations of the world, had in their greatness, combined to form three huge power blocks which controlled all the important matters of everyday life for the world's population, and just about everything else as well.

One of the power blocks was the American Continental Federation, and that included everything from the bottom most tip of Argentina to the deep frozen wastes of Alaska, and all stops in between.

Europe had absorbed everything from eastern Russia to the western Mediterranean, from Iceland down to the Cape of Good Hope in southern Africa, plus any little islands which the European Confederation thought useful or strategic to their needs.

The third power block was composed of all the eastern nations from India through the northern borders of China to Japan, and all stations south, including, surprisingly enough, Australia, despite her mainly European population.

The border between the European and the Eastern block had caused many a skirmish and bloody nose in the past, but at long last a reasonable compromise had been reached, and a sustainable border had been set up which made the old wall of China look like a picket fence.

Long ago Australia had decided to throw her lot in with the Pacific Rim Consortium, as the New America became isolationist in her approach to the other two power groups, and Europe had became more consolidated within itself, from a trade point of view.

The old United Nations had been abandoned when it finally became obvious to all and sundry that it was only equipped with rubber teeth, and had a great propensity to hold long conferences about the 'troubles' instead of waving its big stick and sorting them out.

Trading between the three Super Powers was severely restricted due to heavy tariffs on imports and exports, depending upon who had a surplus and who needed strategic goods and materials.

Coal, crude oil and mineral deposits had been depleted to an alarming level as the general populace demanded an ever bigger slice of the fast dwindling cake, and the disparity between the 'haves' and 'have nots' grew ever wider.

Instead of concentrating their efforts to perfect fusion power, fission power generation along with its subsequent pollution and radiation problems continued to profligate as the materials for fuel fired generators dwindled.

Things came to a bit of a head when one of the 'powers' was caught driving very deep tunnels into its neighbour's territory in order to acquire minerals, as trading for them had failed miserably due to the fact that the transgressor had little to offer in exchange for that which was needed.

As each of the super powers were armed to the teeth with the very latest nuclear weapons, total disaster was narrowly avoided at the last moment by some very hasty shuffle diplomacy and even greater vigilance between them.

Pollution had reached the point where it was adversely affecting the weather systems, on a grand scale. Both ice caps had melted to some degree, and as far as anyone could tell, would continue to do so for some considerable time to come. Many low lying coastal regions were inundated, forcing the local population further inland into an already overcrowded situation, which in turn put an ever increasing burden on the remaining resources.

In one last desperate effort it was decided to try and mine the asteroid belt for minerals, as many small meteorites were rich in metallic ores, and some were of pure metal.

The big race to construct the first space smelting station began. Each nation realized the first to get it up and running would not only gain in prestige, but would also command a high position in the trading league for the metals produced.

The basic idea was to ferry up sections of the smelter station, assembling it in a stationary orbit above each respective nation. The heat would come from giant mirrors, reflecting the sun's undiluted power into a tightly concentrated beam and focusing it onto the smelting hearths of the station. The mirrors would consist of a light alloy frame in a concave dish-like shape, lined with a tough reflective coated plastic.

For once, theory proved to be correct, and the American station was first to be completed, quickly followed by the other two powers. All that was needed to complete the project was a source of materials to smelt, and that was where his predecessors came in.

The space tugs which hunted out the much sought after materials from the asteroid belt were small craft when compared to some of the earlier clumsy attempts of man to get into space, but were plenty powerful enough for the task for which they had been constructed.

Basically they consisted of a very large power source, a small control cabin, an even smaller stores room, and the grappling equipment on the front end.

Before they managed to iron out the bugs in the little craft and develop a safe and reliable technique of capture and retrieval, there weren't too many takers for the job of going out to the asteroid belt, but as time went by, and the need for the materials grew ever more desperate, they finally perfected the tugs, and developed a regime of operation which reduced the odds of failure to an acceptable minimum.

He joined the smelter station tug team at a point in time when there hadn't been a fatality for nearly two years, due mainly to the fact that from the station's point of view, necessity had perfected the system, not so much for the protection of human life, but for the preservation of the precious materials used in the equipment.

He enjoyed the solitary life the job offered. The only time he had to interface with his fellow humans was when he brought in the chunks of asteroid to the smelter station, and that only amounted to the odd haggle over the quality of the retrieved material and the price of provisions for the return journey out to the asteroid belt for the next retrieval.

His one indulgence was the collecting, cutting and mounting of precious and semiprecious stones. He had always felt a fascination for the beauty of cut crystals, and as the journey to the belt took a considerable amount of time, and more to return with his selected asteroid, he was able to spend a considerable amount of time in perfecting his art.

On rare occasions he had even sold some of his creations, and thereby boosted his credit balance to new heights, thus causing a degree of discontent among his fellow pilots, and not a little envy from those who had no skills to speak of.

The source of Cresswell's gemstones came from were the very asteroids he brought back to the smelter station. They were not easy to find, but over the three years he had been engaged in his new occupation, he had learnt what to look for in the way of rock-like bodies, but could only extract those gems which were near the surface.

The retrieval of the stones wasn't without its dangers, as he had to suit up and do a space walk onto the actual rock itself, and this meant leaving the tug behind at a safe distance.

He had just handed over his latest find, a large nickel nugget with an earth mass of some twenty tonnes, and was on his way out again, when the news came through on his communication unit that trouble was brewing back home.

A fission generator situated near the border between the European and the Eastern block had gone critical, melted down its core and everyone had to run for their lives.

As luck would have it, another plant set on the hillside above the stricken generator was processing plutonium, and that melted down at the same time, due to the same cause, a failure in the cooling water supply. This was brought about by the underground reservoir which supplied the water, being surreptitiously tapped by the 'other' group to supplement their supplies.

These two events on their own would have been bad enough, but the Gods were not smiling on Europe that day, and the plutonium meltdown found its way into an underground conduit which led to the lower plant.

When the two meltdowns joined forces, the critical mass of the radioactive materials were well and truly passed, and the ensuing explosion seared the area flat for a radius of eight kilometres, and extinguished all life for a further five, leaving a large crater which later filled up and overflowed with radioactive water.

As the event had happened so quickly, both sides thought the unthinkable, a war between them had begun. It was more by luck than judgement that both sides didn't retaliate against each other. An overhead spy satellite had relayed the pictures down to both sides at the same time. The satellite belonging to one side, the other side having tapped into the satellite's transmissions undetected for years.

Cresswell had heard the news with a degree of sadness, although he despised the greed, cheating and general unpleasantness of life on earth, he felt sorry for those few good people he had come across in his travels. They were, in his estimation, too few to make a marked difference to the conditions which now prevailed on the planet, and he sensed that it would only be a matter of time before things really got out of hand, and that would be the end of mankind.

The space tug had left the smelter station some three days ago, and he had set the automatics for a direct course to the asteroid belt, at least he had his own little world here, although it wouldn't last long when the supplies ran out should the ultimate happen.

After the incident of the radioactive spent fuel container, there was now a long wait for the tug to make the journey out to the shattered remains of what was once a planet, or so the theory went. He wondered if the same fate would befall earth one day. He reset the automatics, took a light snack and decided to sleep awhile.

The dreams came as usual, some based on past experiences, some on wishful thinking and the third category defying all reason. They usually concerned him in some unpleasant disaster from which there was no escape, or he could clearly see the disaster looming ahead and no one would take heed of his warnings. They were only dreams, he thought as he awoke, and worse things were probably happening back on earth, or would do soon if his estimation of events was anything to go by.

He was hungry again, and having satisfied his inner cravings, went up to the main controls to see if everything was going according to plan.

The tug was on course, nothing had been recorded as having been threatening during his sleep period and he had another couple of long shifts to wait out before he would be able to begin his real work.

Although his quarters were cramped, to put it politely, as the designers had given little thought to how the pilots would pass the considerable time on their long journeys, there was just enough room for his gem cutting and polishing equipment.

Cresswell had found a large piece of what he assumed to be amethyst, but he wasn't sure as it was such a deep purple colour, almost black in certain light. He had given much thought as to how he would cut it, and felt almost guilty at the idea of altering such a beautiful work of nature.

The stone was mounted on the cutting table and he advanced the stage towards the fast spinning corrilium cutting wheel. The stone almost sang as the wheel bit in deeply.

Many cuts, a sleep period and five meals later, he had an egg shaped many faceted thing of potential beauty in his hand. It would take many hours of final polishing to realize

the true splendour of his creation, but he knew it was going to be something extra special, and it was with a high degree of excitement that he began the polishing process.

The gem was finished as the tug drew near to the asteroid belt, a pinging warning sound telling him to take over the controls and make the final approach.

Reluctantly he put his equipment away, leaving the now gleaming purple black egg with its shimmering faceted surface on the control table as something new to look at.

Looking into the forward viewing screen he could see the first of the rock lumps which made up the belt. Extra vigilance would now be needed, as not all the asteroids were large and easily observed. The tug had automatically slowed down to a manageable speed for manoeuvring within the belt, and he would have to rely on the particle detection system to warn him of smaller not easily seen stones which could damage the tug, even at these relatively low speeds.

Most of the smaller stones had been swept up by the larger masses as they rotated in their never ending dance around the sun, but there were always a few pieces which had escaped the gravitational pull of the larger rocks, and these had to be avoided at all costs.

He always felt a little surge of excitement whenever he returned to the belt, locating and examining his first rock of the trip. Sometimes he was lucky and found a large ore bearing mass straight away, but often as not, it was a long and tedious job, locating and checking rock after rock for that lucky strike which would boost his credit balance.

Carefully manoeuvring the craft closer to the slowly tumbling mass of space detritus before him, he tried to ascertain what it was composed of. The surface looked rough and jagged, as though it had been made up of a multitude of smaller pieces all crushed together.

The on-board sensors could tell him its mass and density, and approximately its composition, but it would need a space walk to confirm what was actually there, in most cases.

There was always an element of risk in going outside, and although he was used to it, his stomach always turned over a few times whenever he left the tug and jetted across to inspect his latest find. A thin but very strong lifeline was always attached to his belt on these excursions, and it was by this means that he pulled himself back to the craft when he had extracted the necessary information from the asteroid.

Staring intently into the forward viewing screen failed to give him any more data on the mass before him, and the sensors didn't help much either, indicating a much lower mass than he would have expected and a general conglomeration of mixed elements rather than a specific mineral.

There was something different and foreboding about this apparent conglomeration of rocks, and his senses told him to leave it alone, but being the type of person he was, curiosity won over his better judgement and he prepared to leave the safety of the tug to have a closer look at it.

Getting into his space suit was always a chore he disliked. Although the suits had been redesigned and improved many times during his service to the smelter station, he still found it a clumsy contraption, and it restricted his movements far more than he would have liked.

With a small bag of inspection tools attached to his waist belt, he locked the helmet into place, checked the oxygen supply, and muttering under his breath about the cramped conditions of the exit chamber, squeezed into it and pressed the button to pump the air back into the holding tank.

The faint throb of the extraction pump gradually faded as he air was withdrawn from the chamber, and the green light came on to signal that it was safe to open the outer hatch.

There was always a small trace of air left in the chamber, and as the hatch opened it puffed out into space, a twisting little wisp of water vapour to be frozen forever in time.

Giving his life line a sharp tug to make sure it was attached firmly to the hull, Cresswell briefly touched the firing button of the jet pack and felt a gentle push as the exhaust gasses rushed out into space to expand into an ever growing cloud of ultra fine particles, eventually thinning out to invisibility.

The journey across to the asteroid was only a few hundred metres, but it seemed to take forever. Too much forward speed and he would crash into the rocks and possibly damage his suit, so it was of necessity to make haste slowly.

As he drew closer to the surface of the rock formation, the faint sunlight glinted off several shiny points, indicating the possibility of a crystal formation.

Gently squeezing the brake handle of the line reel, he slowed his approach down to arrive feet first on the sinister black mass. There was something about this rock mass which made the hairs on the back of his neck stick up, despite the clamping effect of copious amounts of sweat which had accumulated there.

Carefully he made his way over to what looked like the nearest of the shiny patches he had seen earlier, and bent closer to see what it was. Switching on his hand lamp bathed the area in an intense blue white light, reflecting back from what looked like black volcanic glass embedded in a softer matrix of dark grey foamed pumice.

Withdrawing a blade-like tool from his pouch, he tried to prise the shiny black material from its surrounding bed of pumice, but as the tool cut into the crumbly grey - like mass, he felt rather than heard a faint screeching sound, as though he had cut into a living thing. His hand froze.

For the first time that he could recall, he felt the fear of an alien presence. Something wasn't right here, and his instinct was to back off at once, and leave the rock mass to its own devices. Almost apologetically he withdrew the blade, placing it back in its pouch. He wasn't wanted here, and he knew it in no uncertain terms.

One more quick look around with the hand lamp confirmed his

feelings, it seemed as if the rocks were moving slowly, bunching up around him, trying to hem him in. It might have been his imagination, but he wasn't going to hang around to find out. Taking a firm grip on the safety line, he gave it a tug and the reel automatically wound in the slack as he slowly coasted away from the asteroid and headed back to the homely sanctity of the tug craft.

He could feel his body trembling as he applied the braking thrust from the jet unit, slowing down just in time so as not to crash into the tug. With indecent haste he entered the airlock, slammed the hatch shut and turned on the air supply.

By the time he had entered his quarters and divested himself of the space suit, the trembling had advanced to downright shaking, his whole body seemed to have a vibrating life of its own.

'This is bloody ridiculous.' he mumbled to himself as he sat down at his work bench after heating a beverage bulb and injecting it with a small quantity of illegal alcohol.

A few sucks at the bulb, and the shaking had reduced to a gentle tremble.

'There's never been a recorded encounter with an alien being, ghost or anything else like it, so what the hell was that out there?' The question was rhetorical, and he had long ago given up the consideration that talking to oneself was a sign of madness. All through recorded history there had been stories of unidentified flying objects, right back to biblical times, but no one had ever captured one, let alone talked to its occupants, at least, not when sober.

As far as the experts were concerned, the only known intelligent life was human, although they did concede that it may well exist in other solar systems deep in the Milky Way star clusters.

With one final involuntary shudder, Cresswell gave up trying to rationalize the impossible, and set about the task of searching for another more friendly, or neutral asteroid.

Three shifts and many meals later he came across what looked like the bonanza of the century. It was a massive asteroid, and according to the sensors was composed mostly of nickel ore, and possibly with a solid core of the raw metal, as the mass was far greater than the size implied.

This time he didn't mind donning his suit, and with an almost jaunty air opened the outer hatch, and jetted off towards the huge hulk. There was one problem which he hadn't really faced up to as yet. How was he going to manoeuvre such a large piece of material out of orbit and safely steer it down to the smelter station. And having got it there, how would he stop it from swiping the station out of orbit and wiping out all his carefully saved credits?

Such thoughts were far from his mind as he drifted closer to his prize, adjusting his speed at the last moment so that he landed gently on the surface, taking up the last bit of momentum with bent knees.

Firing an anchor bolt into the surface of the asteroid, he attached his secondary holding line and set about chipping off samples for later analysis back on board the tug. There were none of the unpleasant feelings he had experienced on the first asteroid, and he felt positively cheerful as he went about his tasks.

Having acquired sufficient samples, he loosened the anchor bolt and prepared for the long drift back to the tug. As he was about to push off from the surface, he felt a wash of anguish sweep over him.

'Oh no, not this one as well.' and the bent knees straightened with a whiplash action, propelling his body out into space and at a far higher speed than he had intended.

The line reel fairly sang as it drew in the slackening cord, although he felt the vibration rather than heard the sound.

It took several very careful bursts of the jet to correct his speed as the tug loomed up, and Cresswell hit the hatch door, bouncing off a few metres before the reel took in the last of the line.

Having got back safely inside the tug, he realized that his imagination had got the better of him again, and the asteroid was just a normal chunk of space rock, and he thanked his lucky stars for finding it in the first place.

Opening the analysis unit, he fed in the various samples and waited patiently for the results to be printed out, knowing full well that they would be of high grade ore and would boost his credit balance to new heights.

He might even be able to take a few weeks holiday. But where to? Earth held little for him now, and that only left the recreation centre on board the smelter station. The centre offered the only place in space where one could legally consume alcohol but he wasn't interested in getting blotto.

The only other offering, if one could call it that, were the rather torrid dancing girls and the favours they offered at a price, with little interest and a certain degree of reluctance.

He saw a sample once, and decided they would probably deflate the equipment of a rampant mountain goat without even trying, so that was out.

So what should he do with his hard earned credits? There seemed little to spend them on, for he had all he needed and there wasn't much room for anything else on board the tug.

The data on the analysis unit's screen confirmed his earlier guess, this was indeed a bonanza, and if the whole asteroid was of the same quality with what looked like a solid core, then he was in the money to a serious degree.

Cresswell manoeuvred the tug carefully around to the other side of the asteroid in order to take samples from that area, and just as he was about to leave the communication unit crackled and popped as if someone was trying to get in touch.

He set the unit to automatic frequency search as it was obvious that the standard smelter station frequency was not the one trying to get through.

A series of squeaks, whistles and pops indicated that someone or something was trying to send a signal, but no intelligible speech pattern could be detected.

Switching in a series of filters to cut out the background noise, the squeaks became a little more apparent, but they still made no discernible sense. In one last desperate attempt to try and decipher the broadcast, he tried using the frequency dividers, a thing he had never done before.

As the dividers cut in one after another, the squeaks lowered in pitch until they became a repeating pattern of bleeps, with a time interval between each apparently identical set of sounds.

The only explanation he could think of was that it might be a distress signal of some kind, but like nothing he knew.

It was incumbent upon anyone in space to answer a distress call and render any assistance possible, so the asteroid project would have to be abandoned for the time being.

He angled the tug around so that he could fire a radio marker unit onto the surface, so making it easier to relocate the asteroid again at a later date. It also marked it as his, just in case anyone else might come long and try to claim it, unlikely as that was.

Having made sure the marker beacon was sending its signal out, he set about trying to find the source of the mysterious supposed distress call. The direction finder only gave a faint signal which surprised him, and he followed the course indicated as best he could, the signal fading and returning at regular intervals.

It was several hours later and a good deal deeper into the jumbled mass of the belt, that the distress call became more stable. It was now easier to track, and apart from avoiding the odd rock which loomed up every now and again, he was making good progress towards the source of the signal.

The collision detector emitted its usual scream, warning of something dead ahead and Cresswell slowed the tug to a more manageable velocity just in case the object didn't show up visibly and he crashed into it.

The first thing he saw on the viewing screen was a very large dark mass of what he supposed to be rock, but as he drew nearer it became apparent that it was composed of many pieces of rock, held together by the combined gravitational force of the component parts. The unstable mass was rotating slowly, as if some of the pieces were jockeying for a more favourable position among their companions.

The distress call, if that's what it was, seemed to be coming from a position dead ahead in the middle of the rock jumble, although there was nothing obvious to be seen which could generate such a signal.

He gently brought the craft in closer, and then he saw the faint sunlight glint off what he thought might be a metallic object, half buried in the pile of rotating rocks.

First he would have to match orbit with the asteroid clump, and then very carefully move in to get a better view of what lay trapped in the cluster of cosmic debris.

It was difficult to see any great detail of the entrapped object, as it lay in the shadow of the surrounding rocks, but it certainly looked metallic and manufactured, as opposed to a shiny piece of crystalline rock.

The tug was as close as he dared take it, lest it be caught up in the meat grinder action of the rotating rock mass, so he had no option other than to go across himself to see what it was and render any help if needed.

Checking again that the tug's orbit was as stable as possible with regard to the asteroid, he donned his space suit and released himself out into space, the huge asteroid looming up like a black mass before him.

He was at the limit of his safety line when he touched surface of the rocks, and although it was against all rules and regulations, he knew he would have to release the line and rely on the much shorter secondary line which he usually used to anchor himself while taking rock samples.

As the asteroid rotated, the sunlight suddenly lit up the entrapped metallic object with a blaze of light, catching Cresswell unawares and almost causing him to lose his footing on the unstable rock mass.

'It's definitely manufactured, so therefore must be a craft of some kind.' he muttered to himself, the words distorted as they echoed around inside his helmet.

Slowly and carefully he inched his way down into the cavernous recess where the snub end of the craft stuck out like a distorted thumb.

'Whatever it is, it wasn't made by our lot.' he said to himself as he reached forward and touched the curved shape with his gloved hand. There were deep scars and scratches where the rocks had ground against the hull, denting it in places to a point where the metal had nearly split open.

How much of the craft lay crumpled and trapped within the rock formation, he was unable to tell, but the section of it which protruded suggested that it was a fairly large construction, and far bigger than the tug orbiting the asteroid.

He was nearly at the end of his secondary line when he found what looked like a hatchway into the craft. It was a thick distorted panel of metal, one edge of which was crumpled as though it had been forced up against something unyielding, and had rippled back in a series of ridges.

A narrow gap between the hatch and the main body of the hull allowed him to shine his hand lamp into the interior, lighting up a jumbled tangle of metal struts and broken equipment, none of which was recognizable to him as of earthly origin.

He tried to open the crumpled hatch, but it was stuck fast, only moving a little as he applied the maximum force possible under the circumstances.

Lying just inside, he could make out a long metal bar, and by lying flat up against the hull he was able to grope about inside, his searching gloved fingers eventually grasping the bar and withdrawing.

Using it as a lever, he managed to force the hatch open enough for him squeeze inside, before freeing himself from his secondary line and attaching it to a lug on the inside of the hatch.

It was pitch black in what he thought was the forward cabin or control room, the wandering beam from his lamp lighting up the shattered remains of alien equipment and a horrendous tangle of twisted beams and panels. There was little room to move about freely as the craft had not only been held fast in the rock mass but crushed in a series of cruel grinding gyrations of the entrapping rocks.

'Nothing could live through this.' he said aloud to himself. Cresswell wondered what, if anything, he should say about his find to the authorities back on the smelter station, and then discarded the idea as it was likely to cause a lot of controversy and unwanted attention, after all, they had made their minds up long ago that aliens just didn't exist in this part of the galaxy. He would collect and take back a few pieces of the shattered strange equipment, just for himself.

Something moved. He wasn't sure if it was the random movement of a loose piece of equipment dislodged by the slowly rotating craft, or something else. He had to know for sure that nothing had survived the crushing blows which the alien craft had sustained, and so climbing over the twisted beams which barred his way, he reached the corner and saw his first alien. Or that's what he thought it was.

Whatever it might have been was encased in a helmet of strange alien design, below which appeared to be shoulders and one arm protruding from a mass of tangled wreckage which continued off into the darkness beyond. Cresswell was about to return to the hatchway when the arm moved again in a slow waving motion, trying to attract his attention.

A cold shudder ran down his back. How could anything still be alive in this distorted assortment of beams and equipment was his first thought, and then the urge to render whatever help he could overrode his natural incredulity.

He gently slipped his gloved hand into that of the alien, closing his fingers just enough to let it feel his presence.

The alien hand closed around his, and returned the pressure in a series of feeble squeezes.

'Now what?' he thought, the body was firmly entangled in the wreckage and probably damaged beyond his meagre repair abilities, but he had to make the effort.

Thinking a word or two of comfort wouldn't go amiss, he placed his helmeted head against that of the entrapped alien's and said as loudly as his ears would withstand,

'Don't worry, we'll get you out of here in a jiffy.' and then realized how stupid he sounded. Not only would the alien not be able to understand his words, but it was firmly locked into the surrounding morass of girders and panels, and without a cutting torch and a power jack, he stood little chance of freeing it.

Shining the hand lamp into what he supposed was the visor section of the alien's helmet, he tried to make out the features inside, but could see little detail as the creature had vomited and what could be blood was mixed with it.

He was debating as to whether he should deal a final fatal blow to put the poor creature out of what must have been extreme agony, when the hand which was still clutching his, weakly tried to pull him down again.

As their helmets touched, Cresswell felt rather than heard,

'Can me share with you?' He was startled more than frightened, not sure as to whether he had actually heard it or imagined the alien had spoken. It seemed to ring in his head, as though he had spoken the words himself.

'Yes of course you can, I'll get you back to my craft in no time at all.' he answered automatically.

After that, he now felt compelled to help more than ever, so he touched helmets again gently and said 'I'll get you out of here somehow, it might be painful, but I'll do it.' If he could hear the alien, then it could hear him.

The craft gave a violent shudder and a mass of equipment slid slowly, dream like, across the floor, pushing him before it and pinning the creature down even more firmly.

Fixing the hand lamp to the tacpad on his chest, he set about removing all the lose debris from around the alien body and discovered that only two main pieces of metal really held it pinned down.

The first piece gave way to his persistent levering with the bar he had opened the hatch with, while the second one took a little more effort and he was beginning to sweat up in his suit as the end of the restraining beam finally gave way and slid to one side.

The legs of the alien were horribly twisted and disjointed, or maybe that's how they were meant to be, he didn't know, but they straightened out as he dragged the broken body by the shoulders towards the partly open hatchway.

Cresswell felt he must have done even more damage to the alien as he dragged it through the small opening, but as there had been no further movement from it since he had freed it from the wreckage, he assumed it was unconscious and therefore wouldn't feel any pain.

Untying the secondary line from the lug on the hatch, he attached it to the alien and then proceeded to drag it out of the cave-like recess in the rock pile to the point where he had attached his main safety line.

The alien was either very flexible and jointed differently to humans, or its skeleton had been shattered from the impacts received from the debris within the space craft. in the ever moving rock pile.

He attached the main line to the reel on his belt, held the alien body under one arm and pushed off into space, eager to regain the safety of the tug.

The reel greedily took up the slack as the pair travelled towards the distant tug, and a deep sigh of relief whistled around the inside of Cresswell's helmet as he made contact with a more familiar craft, and opened the entry hatch.

It was a very tight squeeze getting the alien in with him, as the cubicle was only designed for one, but he made it, just.

As he laid the crumpled body down on the floor of his cabin and straightened out the limbs as he thought they should be, he realized just how tired he was. Every muscle ached, his heart was pounding and he was soaking wet.

There seemed little he could do for the alien as he didn't know if the air in his ship would be poisonous to it, and he didn't have much in the way of medical supplies anyway.

He felt he should do something, but what? He checked to see if there was any movement he could detect when he tapped on the alien's helmet or moved its arms, but it just lay there, as inert as the rest of the fixtures and fitting.

Had he saved its life? There was no way of telling that he could think of. Perhaps he had better just let it rest there, and see if it responded to his signals later on.

Strangely, he felt hungry, but this body was crying out for rest and he thought it might be a good idea to lie down for a few minutes before doing anything else, just to let his tortured muscles relax a little.

The next thing he knew was that seven hours had passed, his body still ached and he was now ravenously hungry.

Greedily sucking on a liquid food bulb, he looked down at the alien, but somehow it looked different, and then he realized what it was. The suit was fully extended as if the internal air pressure had increased.

My God, I hope it doesn't burst.' he muttered to himself as he reached down to readjust one of the arms, and was shocked to find that there appeared to be no bones now, It was just a rubber like tube filled with something liquid, and made a sloshing sound as he let it go in surprise.

Quickly checking the rest of the body, he nearly brought up the contents of the food bulb as he realized that the whole thing had turned to a gel like liquid, all the bones having disintegrated. He was now sure the alien was as dead as one could get without being incinerated, but what should he do with it? He didn't like the idea of taking it back to the smelter station because of all the trouble it could bring about trying to explain what he had done and why. There were too many people with very fixed ideas who would stop at nothing to protect their concepts of the universe, and he didn't feel like challenging any of them, even with the proof of a body.

But was it proof? It was just a rubber like suit filled with some strange liquid. No, he wasn't going to get tangled up in that kind of fracas.

He couldn't keep it indefinitely on board the tug, and what would be the point anyway? Put it back in the alien ship?

That was too risky, it was bad enough trying to get it out. No, the only alternative was to launch it into space in as respectful a manner as possible. This he resolved to do during the next watch, just in case by some miracle it came back to life, or did something other than just lay there.

A sudden thought occurred to him, 'What's the position of the tug?' quickly he moved over to the control panel and read the data. The tug had moved a little closer to the asteroid mass, and given enough time it would have been captured by it and been ground to pieces like the alien ship.

'But what the hell could have caused that?' he muttered.

'That damn thing must have something very solid in there somewhere to generate that much gravity.'

Checking on the mass detector proved the point, the mass of the conglomeration of rocks was way above what it should have been according to his experienced guess, so there was something very dense in there somewhere.

The mystery mass tickled his curiosity, and he was tempted for a moment to try and find out what it was, but then the dangers of such an expedition without a companion to extricate him if needed, made it totally non-viable.

Cresswell felt saddened that he hadn't been able to rescue the alien, but he had given it his best shot and that was the most he could have done.

There was little point in delaying the inevitable, so he dragged the liquefied body over to the hatch entrance, and taking one last look into the now completely obscured helmet in the vain hope that he could gain some information from its sad occupant, he pushed it into the chamber and then squeezed in himself.

The air was sucked out of the chamber to the accompanying throb of the extraction pump, and it seemed to take nearly twice as long as usual. The green light came on, and he opened the outer hatch to the deep blackness of space with its pinpoint spattering of diamond like stars.

He paused for a moment, wishing that things could have been different and then gave the limp body a firm push, sending it spinning out towards the stars, from which it no doubt came.

He wondered about giving a salute, but thought it inappropriate somehow, so just mouthed 'Goodbye' and wished he could get at his face to wipe away the tears which were stinging his eyes. He closed the hatch, feeling strangely reluctant to do so and returned to the main cabin, aware of an odd feeling of loneliness.

There was nothing more he could do here, although he was still intrigued by the high gravitational pull of the asteroid clump, he knew better than to tackle it on his own.

Cresswell turned the tug away from the enigmatic collection of rocks and set course for the asteroid with the marker beacon he had found earlier. He knew he should check it's mass again to be sure that the tug could handle such a large object as it was certainly bigger than anything he had attempted before. There were set limits to the amount of mass the tug could handle, and the instruments would warm him if he chose to exceed them.

The tug picked up the marker beacon's signal, and began the long journey back. There was little to do except for a few small course corrections as he dodged the odd rogue rock, leaving him plenty of time to think over the events of the last few hours. He played over many different scenarios which could have taken place if he had taken the alien back to the smelter station, and each of them seemed to indicate more trouble than they were worth. He still had difficulty in reconciling the fact that despite all of man's scientific advances, as a race they were still hide-bound by many stuck and outdated ideas.

Eventually the dark shape of the marked asteroid loomed up ahead, the ship's control panel gave a loud 'ping' to announce its presence and he readied himself for the task of capture, and the more difficult one of dragging the huge lump of mineral down to the smelter station.

As he suspected, the mass was a little over the limit the tug was designed to handle, and the instruments advised him of this. It was within his power to over ride the mass limit by some twenty per cent, but above that the tug would automatically refuse to co-operate, although it had never done so to him. But then, he had never managed to find such a large amount of high grade ore in one piece before.

First Cresswell had to line the tug up, locate a point where the rock looked stable, and fire in a tow bolt.

The tug gave a small shudder as the bolt was released under extreme pressure from its launch tube, and continued to accelerate until it made contact with the rock surface.

The specially designed head then received another boost in speed from a shaped charge in its tail, driving it deeply into the rock, the tip expanding out to lock it firmly in place.

The first time he had used one of these bolts, he felt doubtful of its efficiency, and was gentle in the extreme when putting the tug into towing mode. He still felt surprised each time the bolts held when the tug took up the strain.

Having secured the towing bolt to the surface of the asteroid, the tug was manoeuvred into position, the long towing cable payed out and the even longer pull began.

The principle behind the operation was to tow the asteroid against its direction of rotation, thus reducing the centrifugal force which kept it circling the sun in a reasonably stable orbit. The gravitational pull of the sun, though weak at this distance, would help a little in bringing the asteroid down to an orbit close to the smelter station, where it was then parked in a stable orbit until needed.

The theory was basically simple, the power needed to accomplish this feat was considerable, and only paid off when the ore was of a high enough grade. Cresswell was quite convinced that his latest catch would set him up for life, if he could get it back safely.

The on-board computer would work out the trajectories and the thrust needed, applying it so as to conserve enough fuel for the slow down when earth orbit was neared. He could always call for assistance for the parking orbit, but would have to pay for it.

The only really difficult part of the journey home was leaving the asteroid belt itself. The occasional rogue rock could come cruising along and get in the way. The tug could avoid such things, but when towing a large piece of asteroid it made life a little more difficult, and dangerous.

Only once before had he needed to release the tow to avoid a medium sized space rock, and picking up the tow again meant a journey outside to physically pick up the end of the cable and get it back to the tug. I wasn't one of his favourite occupations.

The journey down to earth orbit was long and boring, many crystals had been cut, polished and mounted by the time the tug began it's long deceleration process, and that seemed to take forever.

At long last the smelter station could be picked out as a bright pinpoint of light, or at least, its massive array of reflectors could. The fuel reserves were dangerously low, and deep inside he knew he would have to call for help in the final parking manoeuvre, and that meant losing some of his catch in assistant fees.

The station personnel were an astute bunch of crooks, and they could work out to the last gram how much fuel they would have to expend, and how much they could soak him for the service.

In reality, he had no option. If he couldn't park the asteroid himself and he wouldn't accept help, it would have to be abandoned, and then someone else with a power tug would claim it as a free moving item of space flotsam.

Cresswell now knew he had an unmentionable part of his anatomy held firmly in the vice like grip of the station's more unscrupulous members, but had to swallow hard and accept the fact. The call went out for assistance, and the haggling began, not that he had much say in the matter. If you have the only taxi in town, you can call the tune as to the fare, as long as you're not too silly, and they weren't.

An agreement was reached, he would have to say goodbye to about twenty per cent of the asteroid's value, but that still left a considerable amount for his piggy bank.

Two large power tugs hove into view a couple of hours later and attached their towing cables, braced themselves and began the last part of the parking orbit.

He had to admit, these boys knew their job, and not one drop of fuel was wasted by them.

The huge block of mineral was parked, for want of a better word, the assistant tugs disengaging their tow lines and leaving a somewhat sore Cresswell to unhitch his own.

The haggling with the smelter station assayers would now commence, and that could also prove to be traumatic as they would want to get the best deal possible without encouraging Cresswell to take his wares to either of the other two smelters.

He released the tow cable from the asteroid, moved his tug over to the parking bay of the smelter and went aboard.

The whole place had a hard smell to it, something metallic and dusty, or was it his dislike for the station? He wished he could have done the deal without leaving his ship, but the only way to get a decent price was to face the buyers in person, and show them what a tough hard-nosed little sod he was, which he wasn't really.

Having checked in at the reception desk, Cresswell made his way to the refreshment area for a good meal, cooked or processed by someone else for a change. The menu looked quite appetizing, and he made a careful selection of things he didn't have on board the tug before going over to a table near a viewing port, so that he could watch the activity of others for a change.

He was just getting interested in the pitiful antics of an inept crew trying to get a service module out to one of the giant mirror complexes, when a miserable looking woman with a scruffy crew cut and a pallid face to match, dumped a large plateful of food before him.

He looked down at the unhappy offering in front of him, looked up at the serving wench, and proceeded to give his undiluted opinion on the culinary skills and lack of artistic presentation of the offending mess before him.

As he paused to draw breath for another blast, the waitress gave him a broken toothed contorted smile, bobbed her head, spun on her heels and made off to the serving bar, her greasy grey over sized coveralls trying to keep pace with her mincing footsteps, where she no doubt added Cresswell's comments to those of his predecessors.

'God, standards have fallen even lower since last time.' he said to no one in particular, but he was hungry, and after a few mouthfuls had to admit it didn't taste too bad after all, it just looked foul.

The meal finished, he decided that the inevitable could no longer be put off, and made his way to the Assayer's office.

'Well, you've got a fair old lump of ore out there this time, Cresswell.' the older of the two uniformed Assayers said with a knowing grin.

'Yes, and it's got a solid core, as I expect you've already found out,' he replied, 'so don't get any ideas about trying to fob me off with just the ore content.'

'Would we do a thing like that to someone who keeps us supplied with some of the best ores obtained for the belt?'

'I'm sure you would, if you thought for one moment you'd get away with it.' Cresswell replied with a matching, knowing grin.

The false smiles left the faces of the Assayers as if they had been turned off like a tap, to be replaced with the look of grim determination only a good negotiator can muster.

'Right, let's cut the crap and get down to business.' the elder one said. 'You have something we want, namely a very large mass of high grade ore, and we have something you want, credits for your old age, if you ever reach it.'

The younger Assayer clumsily riffled through some documents on the desk, tapped the keys of his computer for a moment, and after a furtive glance at its screen, slyly added,

'The mass has been calculated at fourteen thousand tonnes, for which we can pay you at the rate of seventy two credits per tonne. This amounts to a little over one million credits.

'We can offer one million flat, and we take a chance on the supposed solid core of the mass.'

'But that core might be solid nickel,' he exclaimed, exasperation already showing in his voice.

'And again, it might not.' the elder one said, with an air of finality in his voice.

'I'm sure I can get a better price for it at either of the other two stations.' Cresswell said confidently, knowing he could, and then sat back in his chair to let them think that one over.

'Of course you could my friend, but take into account the fact that you already owe about one fifth of it's value to the assistant tugs you had to call up to park the asteroid, and you would lose about the same, or perhaps a little more knowing the predicament you are in, if you employed them again to get the ore across to either of the other two smelters.' The elder Assayer sat back also, knowing he was winning the argument so far.

Cresswell thought about the situation carefully. He would probable gain very little by going elsewhere, and there was always the risk of something going wrong with such a big asteroid, or being engineered to do so. He resigned himself to having to accept the offer, but not before he made them sweat a little more first.

'I think it only fair to tell you two sharks,' he continued, hoping they didn't put his statement to the test, 'that the American smelter has already unofficially offered me seventy eight credits per tonne, and they will tow it away for free.'

'They may well do, but they'll have to pay us a levy first, as it's parked in our space.'

'I thought you might come up with that one,' Cresswell wasn't going to give up that easily, 'and I've already estimated that I could still come out a little way ahead of your offer, despite your sharp practices.'

'Maybe you could, maybe you couldn't. But is it worth the risks involved? Come on Cresswell, we'll give you an extra half credit per tonne to show our good nature, and that's the final offer, take it or leave it.' Both Assayers sat back with a look of stony determinism on their faces, and waited for Cresswell to give up the unequal struggle.

He could see there was little more to be gained from the discussion, and he knew he didn't dare call their bluff any more as they could make things very awkward for him not only now, but in the future.

'All right, that seems a little more fair.' he wasn't going to give in with any grace if he could help it.

'I'll accept your offer this time, but bear in mind there is another big one out there, and next time I'll get an assessment on it before I park.' He hoped that last remark left them feeling just a little bit uneasy.

The printer spat out an agreement form with the details of the deal set out in very clear terms, and Cresswell signed and thumb-printed it before reluctantly shaking hands with the two Assayers and leaving the room.

At least the asteroid was off his hands, and its safe keeping was not his responsibility any more.

He recalled a tale which went the rounds a few years ago about a particularly rich but small asteroid which went missing while the price negotiations were going on. It had been signed for, and the credits transferred to the tug man.

When they gleefully went to do another inspection of their prize, it had vanished. It nearly caused a war between the smelter stations, and that would have spread down to earth.

Whether the story was true or not he didn't know, but he liked to think it was, and longed for the day when he could participate in such a scheme.

He was hungry again after his struggle to get reasonable recompense for his asteroid, and not fancying another visit to the depressing general refreshment salon, he thought it was about time he got the score evened up a little, and went to the reception area.

Going up to the main desk, he asked if the Tug Master could spare him a few moments of his precious time, and after the hatchet-faced individual behind the desk had faffed about and mumbled incoherently into his phone, it was agreed that he should go up to the highly exalted office of the Tug Master, if that suited him. It did.

As Cresswell went deeper into the complex, the furnishings and fittings grew ever more palatial, until he paused before the grand splendour of the Tug Master's door.

The basic tugs were the property of the smelter station, and were only on loan, but one could, if one wished, pay a premium and get issued with a more luxuriously appointed one. Cresswell had no real need or desire for such, as they had no more room in them than the standard model, all the extra space being taken up with so called luxury items and gimmicks.

But if he showed an interest in one?

He knocked, and the door swung open of its own volition.

'Do come in Cresswell, I hear you've had a stroke of luck lately.' It was a statement, rather than a question from the Tug Master.

'Yes, I have rather,' he replied, 'and it looks as if I shall have another one shortly. I was on my way to have a meal before returning to the belt, when I thought it might be an idea to get some information on the tug upgrades.'

Credit signs lit up in the Tug Master's eyes, and his smile threatened to split his face in two.

'It would be my pleasure, Cresswell, I was about to have a bite to eat myself, so perhaps we can crack two nuts with one blow, as it were, and discuss the matter over a meal?'

'That would be nice.' replied Cresswell, his smile being mainly due to the fact that the bait had been taken, and a decent meal was now in the offing.

The senior staff restaurant was a thing of legend, and very few of the 'lower lives' had even managed to get their noses in, let alone eaten there. Tug men were considered even lower, almost alien, and to be taken for a ride and chiselled out of their rights at every opportunity. Cresswell was feeling very pleased with himself, and would feel even more so after the impending meal.

The room itself was a thing of splendour. Glowing drapes of fine fabrics adorned the walls, while a beamed ceiling arched overhead in a series of graceful curves. Crystal hung light fittings suspended from the top of each domed section glittered and tinkled as the gentle draft of purified air swept in and around the room.

'I could happily eat here every day.' thought Cresswell, as he was courteously ushered to a vacant table.

A smartly dressed waiter appeared out of nowhere and bobbed his head respectfully as he removed Cresswell's chair, and then gracefully slid it under him, while another did the same for the Tug Master.

A menu board was passed to each of them, and his eyes nearly gave the game away as he looked down the long list of almost forgotten delicacies.

Having made their choice of main meal the waiters hurried away, leaving Cresswell to bluff out the interval before the exotic dishes would be produced.

'We have several models to choose from, in varying degrees of luxurious appointment.' was the Tug Master's opening gambit, a series of gaudy coloured data cards appearing in his hand.

'Perhaps you would like to look at some while we wait for our meal?'

He took them with his best smile, and thumbed through the sheets.

'They are rather splendid.' he said at last, trying to give an apparency of genuine interest.

'I must say, this one in particular is very attractive, and seems to have a holographic projector included.'

'Er, well the projector, as you can see, is slightly 'greyed out', and is therefore an optional extra.'

Cresswell couldn't see any 'greying out' of the projector, and put it down to the Tug Master trying to up the anti, and wring as much as possible from the deal.

'And how much extra would that be?' he asked, trying not to let his assessment of the Tug Master show, which was getting more difficult with the passage time.

'Oh, only a mere five hundred credits if you put down a fifty per cent deposit on the whole ship, otherwise I'm afraid it would amount to nearly a thousand extra.'

Luckily the meal arrived, and he tucked in, trying to hide the fact that he was not usually accustomed to such great delicacies.

Two more courses arrived, the last being of exotic fruits the likes of which Cresswell had never heard of, let alone tasted. He realized that he could very easily get used to this kind of eating, if he wasn't careful. Most of the items in the meal weren't even available from the food stores used by the tug men or general station staff, mainly he supposed because of the cost involved.

The meal drew to a close, and the terminating beverage arrived. It was a fruity drink, and very easy on the palate.

After taking a few sips, he realized that it probably contained a large quantity of alcohol as his head felt a little woozy, and more than likely was part of the softening up process aimed at encouraging him to pay the premium on a super tug.

'Well, what do you think Cresswell?   Someone of your stature should have a premium tug, as it sets you above the general run of the mill tug men, and lets face it, you are in that position already, so why not show it?'

He selected two of the super tug data sheets and said, 'May I take these with me? I think I shall have to give it a little more thought before I finally decide which one I have, after all it's a very large outlay.'

The Tug Master beamed, he had hooked another customer, and it would only be a matter of time before his credit balance went up another few thousand notches.

The meeting was closed affably, each having attained what they set out to get, and they went their separate ways, Cresswell going back down through the less opulent levels of the station towards the lower tug bay, and his standard issue tug.

Reaching the docking bay level, he decided to visit the luxury store and treat himself to a little indulgence after the recent windfall of the asteroid, after all, he could well afford it now, and a few hundred credits would make little difference to his overall balance.

It was halfway along one of the darker twisting passageways that he felt rather than heard footsteps behind him. A sudden flush of foreboding overcame him and a shudder went down his back, followed by a sense of disorientation and a dream like state.

Before he knew what had happened, he had dropped to a low crouching position, spun around to face the way he had come, and then leapt upward and forward, his arms straight out before him, hands locked together.

There was a sickening crunch as his locked hands made contact under the jaw of the person before him, its head snapping back with the sound of a breaking stick.

As the stricken body fell to the floor, he spun around, his right leg lashing out like a scythe and bringing the other would be assailant crashing to the ground.

Before he could stop himself, he had gripped its head, raising the body from the ground, and given it a whip like shake, the sharp crack which followed told him he would have no further trouble from that source.

The strange dream like feeling went as quickly as it had come, and he felt normal again. Looking down at the two bodies before him, he realized that if he hadn't done what he had, he wouldn't have been doing any more tug work for a while, if ever.

One of the assailants still had a cosh like instrument locked firmly in his hand, while the other one had an illegal stun-gun in his still twitching grip. Obviously he wasn't intended to go asteroid hunting, or anything else for that matter.

Two things worried him. Who would sanction such a pointless affront on his person? Unless of course, the transfer of his credits had been delayed somehow, and if he wasn't around to query the lack of funds they could be siphoned off to someone else's account. But he had never heard of such a thing happening before.

The other thing which he couldn't explain was the fact that he had reacted in such a fashion, without actually knowing what was about to occur, and it was all over in one terminal flash-like motion, irrevocable, cold and unemotional.

He had never taken a life before, let alone two, but he didn't feel any remorse for what he had done, and that didn't seem right either.

Cresswell stood rooted to the spot for a moment.

How had he known that two men were about to attack him, he hadn't even heard them, and if he had, they might have just been perfectly innocent station staff. So why did he spin around and go in for the kill without even thinking about it?

There was something very unnerving about the whole incident and it left him feeling strangely different somehow.

Reporting the incident would only cause more problems, and he would be asked for an explanation of his actions, which he couldn't comprehend as yet.

Leaving the two defunct and twisted bodies in the corridor, he hurried along to the store, half-heartedly selecting a few items for his creature comforts on the next journey out, and then headed for the docking bay. Pausing on his way, he spent a little time looking at a display cabinet showing the latest in entertainment discs, but none took his fancy at the moment, and he hurried along towards the more familiar surroundings of his homely ship.

The tug had been refuelled, restocked with food stuffs, and the extras he had ordered had deposited in the cabin.

'Amazing how quickly people can respond when a few credits are involved.' he thought as he checked the manifest and put the items away in their respective compartments.

Sealing the outer hatch, he felt better about the various happenings of the last few hours, cheering himself up a little by thinking of the sumptuous meal he had conned out of the Tug Master at no cost to himself.

He called in on the communication channel for clearance to leave the station, announcing his intention to return to a specific section of the belt for further asteroid acquisition. They liked to know where their tugs were going in case there was a mishap, as they could then at least rescue their property.

Clearance came, and he released the holding clamps, the little tug easing forward into the velvet black of space, and then it surged forward on the next mission and the restful solitude he craved.

There was little to do after setting the auto pilot, and he relaxed back in his 'Super Comfort' chair with its infinitely variable settings, one of the few luxuries he had treated himself to on a previous large find from the belt.

Things were getting worse, as far as he could tell from the meagre information he was able to obtain. News from earth was well censored, they only let you know what they thought fit for your consumption, but he could read between the lines, and didn't like what he found

The stresses between the three great super powers were ever on the increase, mainly caused by unequal sharing of the earth's resources, and exacerbated by unscrupulous dealings between the main raw material suppliers.

The few un-syndicated countries which still existed were having a really hard time of it, as the main power blocks were forever squeezing them for what little resources they had left, their independence costing them dearly as they struggled to survive.

One such country had been found hoarding a considerable quantity of biological weaponry, some of which had been recently made, and was hard put to explain it away.

Before they could come up with a good excuse for their sins, they were 'taken over' very swiftly, demilitarised, de-commercialised and to some extent depopulated, as many of the higher echelon had disappeared without trace. In effect, the country had ceased to exist, being absorbed into the neighbouring power block.

Two:
Out of Hiding

CRESSWELL FORGOT ABOUT the turbulent conditions back on his home planet and those of the smelter stations as he put his attention on the occupation of gem cutting.

By the time the tug gave it's warning 'ping' to tell him that they were nearing the belt, he had cut, polished and mounted several new stones to his satisfaction, and wondered if he could earn a good living at it instead of the somewhat hazardous occupation of asteroid hunting.

The chance of finding another monster asteroid like the one he had recently delivered to the smelter station, was fairly remote, but the temptation to look was there.

Cresswell, having made a few calculations, realized that he didn't really need to work much longer in order to live out the rest of his life quite comfortably, but the main problem was where to do so. He didn't fancy earth, to put it mildly, but there was nowhere else, unless he just stayed in space on board a tug-like vessel. He concluded that he might as well continue to work as it occupied his time between gem cutting, so giving a variety of interests to life.

Using the long range scanner, he searched the depths of the belt for likely objects to inspect, and located a cluster of shapes deep within the first of the main bands of debris.

In the outer ring, there was plenty of space between the asteroids, and navigation was easy, but as one went deeper, the number of celestial objects grew in number per cubic kilometre, and some were unstable in their orbits as they jockeyed for position, the gravity of the larger masses affecting the smaller ones.

The cluster he was now heading for was positioned within the unstable area, and he would have to be very careful not to hit one of the smaller pieces of rock as they wove their way around the system, also they were difficult to locate because of their small mass.

Cresswell had nearly reached his target area when he realized he was very tired, and noted with some surprise that he had been continually on watch for fifteen hours. He was reaching a point of reduced efficiency, which was dangerous in the extreme.

The only way he could take a break was to park the tug in orbit with the rest of the belt, so that they all circled the sun at the same pace, and hope that no rogue rock came flying in from an unexpected direction.

The tug was lined up with the nearest large asteroid, the automatics switched on to keep it so, and the range of the object warning unit was increased to maximum.

After a meal, he felt a little refreshed, but decided that a good sleep was the most sensible thing to do.

Snuggling down in his sleep pod with its soft fleecy coverings, he was soon into deep sleep, dreaming dreams of large asteroids of solid gold and a very angry Tug Master paying an astronomical amount for an enormous meal Cresswell had just eaten.

He was rudely awakened from his slumbers by the persistent warning sound of the object detector. Something was approaching the tug, and he leapt out of the sleep pod and almost ran the few steps to the control desk.

The screen was at its highest magnification and showed a symmetrical shape slowly edging its way towards the tug. As far as he knew, no one else had been given the all clear to be in this area, or anywhere nearby.

Opening up the communication unit, he switched it to sweep all usable frequencies in turn, and sent his message,

'Who are you? Do you need help?'

There wasn't even a whisper back from the object, which continued to close the distance between them, just the faint hiss of static, which was the normal background noise.

Cresswell felt a new feeling of unease, similar to that he had experienced back on the smelter station.

Something wasn't right, and he was very vulnerable out here in space, no weapons and no one to call upon for help should he need it.

There was something sinister about the dark object, which, as it drew nearer, took on the unmistakable shape of a tug ship, slowly rotating as if out of control.

Once more he sent out his message, but there was still no reply, but far more worrying were the faint flecks of light showing from its lateral jets as the object stopped spinning, and that meant someone was on board, and in control.

While locked in the paralysing shock of what this implied, he saw the mystery craft alter course slightly and it was now pointing directly at Cresswell.

Instinctively he engaged the reverse thrust which was used for towing asteroids, and eased the craft out of alignment, waiting to see what would happen next.

He didn't have long to wait, the mystery tug swung around so that it was pointing in his direction again, and accelerated.

Cresswell saw two courses of action open to him. Stay and fight it out, but with what? Or run. But the other craft looked the same as his and would be powered with the same type of propulsion unit. Their speeds would be virtually the same, so there was no chance of out running the other tug.

A surge of blind panic swept over him and he knew a new kind fear, the sort which caused one to go icy cold and sweat at the same time, while his heart hammered in his chest like an old engine with a badly worn bearing.

Perhaps he could hide or dodge the other craft by going into a dense cluster of asteroids, a sort of deadly hide and seek, but he would need to get a head start on the craft.

Without realizing he had done so, he had backed the tug again, and swung it around in a curve, it was better than just being a sitting target.

Desperately he searched the forward screen for a collection of asteroids in which he could hide for a while, giving him a chance to figure out a way of staying alive, and if possible, defeating his adversary as he now deemed it to be.

In the top left corner of the screen there was cloudy patch, only just within range of the scanners. If he could make it there and it was a group of large rocks, he stood a chance.

Cresswell veered the tug around in an arc, trying to get on the blind side of the other vessel's scanners, and then made his frantic bid for the rock cluster. He didn't dare use full speed this deep in the belt, but he wasn't far off it as the little craft streaked for cover in the asteroid cluster.

As he neared his goal, the rear view screen showed an occasional flash of light as the weak rays of the sun glittered on the following craft, and he knew he hadn't made that much headway on his opponent's vessel, or his opponent had taken a greater risk than he had, and used full power. Someone was out to terminate him, that was now obvious.

The kill or be killed ethos was something he had never really contemplated, but there was now no option, and his determination level rose to new heights.

Guiding the tug in between the rocks was no mean feat under normal circumstances, but at speed and someone with nasty intentions on your tail, it was the ultimate horror.

He grazed two smaller rocks as he manoeuvred into the tumbling mass of asteroids, and finally positioned the tug alongside a large grey lump of what looked like foamed pumice, nearly twice the size of the tug.

Hiding in the shadow side, he waited to see what would transpire. Would the assailant have the nerve to follow him into such a dangerous situation? Or would he just stay and wait for him to lose his nerve and make a run for it?

The minutes ticked by, seeming like hours, and then there was a glint of light off something metallic as the assailant's tug nosed into the tumbling rock mass.

There was a small but bright flash of blue white light as the approaching tug fired its anchor bolt mechanism, the long thin cable just visible as a flickering strand of light coming towards him.

For the second time, Cresswell froze in horror as he realized what was about to happen. The bolt would have enough momentum to pierce the hull, and then the explosive charge, which was intended to drive the bolt home into an asteroid, would explode, reducing the contents of the tug into tiny fragments, him included. The woozy feeling came over him again, and he almost felt relieved as the fear seemed to evaporate.

Cresswell watched fascinated in an almost dream like state, as his body seemed to take control over things of its own volition. His left hand flew out to the controls, briefly touching the forward propulsion button, and the little tug responded by slipping backwards a few metres and then stopping as the rear unit was pulsed.

The anchor bolt with its cable flashed by, missing the hull by a few millimetres, the cable sending a nerve tingling scraping sound reverberating throughout the tug as it rasped across the outer skin of the craft.

Before he could stop himself, he had grabbed one of the flexible water containers, slipped it into the microwave, spun around in one fluid motion scooping the fleecy sleeping cover up in the other hand. With the now hot water container wrapped in the fleece, he quickly slipped into his space suit and entered the exit chamber, holding the fleece wrapped container to his chest as if his life depended upon it.

It took forever for the pump to extract all the air from the chamber, but finally the outer door opened, and he drifted out into the blackness of space.

The anchor bolt had embedded itself into the pumice like rock, and he arrived to land gently a few metres away from the firmly attached bolt. Holding onto the rough surface, he managed to pull his body along to the protruding bolt and watched in bewilderment as his hands pushed the fast cooling container of water out of its covers and released the top. As the water left the container under the pressure of a hard squeeze, it evaporated in a cloud of water vapour, but some of it reached the surface of the bolt unit, and froze into a solid sparkling white lump.

He then realized the purpose of the exercise, the ice would jam the release mechanism, so preventing the assailant from disconnecting the unit, thus leaving the tug and rock joined together, one at each end of a very long cable.

But how had he known how to do this? Was it just a basic instinct, driven by sheer necessity, or was there something else guiding his hand, like the Gods of old? In the dream-like state in which he seemed to float, he found it very difficult to think coherently, and gave up as he found his body returning to the safety of the tug.

He didn't remember getting on board again, he just found himself watching as the tug edged slowly forward and set its nose into a depression on the surface of the pumice rock.

The rear propulsion came on, and the pair accelerated forwards in a gentle curve, using the stationary assailant's tug as a centre point of rotation.

Cresswell could feel himself being pulled sideways as the velocity increased until the propulsion cut off, and they were floating freely in space once more.

The rock continued its journey, the assailants craft now joining in the heavenly dance as the two gyrated around a shared centre of rotation.

The assailant was now irrevocably doomed, as no matter how it tried to out manoeuvre the attached rock, it couldn't cancel the momentum imparted to it by Cresswell's tug, and sooner or later the cable would snag on something and then proceed to wind itself around the tug, with the attached rock increasing in velocity as its radius of gyration decreased. In the end, the rock would smash into the tug, imparting its stored momentum in a final burst of devastating energy.

He found himself sitting at the controls, shaking, bathed in sweat, and all his muscles aching. His vision had cleared, and as far as he could tell, he was in control again.

Bit by bit, the reality of what had just happened dawned upon him, and he knew beyond doubt he wasn't alone.

'All right, who and what are you.' he called out, not really expecting an answer.

'*Do not be afraid,*' the voice echoed in his head as it had done back on the crushed alien craft so long ago, '*I share with you, as you gave your consent when you tried to rescue my body. I am sorry to take your body over in times of crisis when you seem unable to act, but it is important that your body survives, for we both share it now.*'

Somehow, he wasn't as surprised as he thought he should be, thinking back to the attack he suffered on the smelter.

'But how can you share my body, I've never heard of such a thing before? Surely I would feel something?'

'*I choose to stay in the background until I am needed. Together we can survive better, as I have faster response times, but your body will suffer a little strain in its muscles when I move it too quickly. If it is your absolute wish that I leave your body, then I must do so, but I will be marooned here in your system. If we stay together, then I stand a chance of rescue by my people at some time in the future. You must choose what happens, for what I have done is not ethically correct among my people, nor yours I suspect.*'

This was a little more than Cresswell had expected, and it took him a while to gather his thoughts together, and reach the only conclusion he could.

'From what has happened, I can't deny that I wouldn't have survived without your help, so I owe you something, and there is little else I can offer than to let you 'share' with me, as you put it.'

There was a mental silence for a few moments as he watched the gyrations of the assailant's tug and the asteroid.

The pilot was desperately trying to dissipate the energy stored up in the spinning rock, and failing miserably. Each time he accelerated the tug in a direction to pull the pumice mass out of its orbit around the tug he became more desperate, got it wrong, and added to the inevitable moment when the tow line would catch on something and the big wrap around would commence.

'*I sense you feel sorry for your antagonist.*' Cresswell was jerked out of the hypnotic trance of watching the dancing pair in the viewing screen.

'Yes, I don't like the idea of taking another person's life.'

'*But he would have taken yours, with no doubts.*'

'I know that, but it still doesn't make it right.'

At long last the towing cable must have caught on something to do with the main propulsion unit and either bent it, or damaged it in some way, for the tug was now completely out of control, spinning and jerking about like a demented puppet with severe colic.

And then came the inevitable moment from which there was no recourse, the cable was visibly winding itself around the tug, the asteroid spinning faster and faster around it as the radius of gyration decreased. The final contact came in a soundless explosion of metallic fragments and a flash of brilliant light as the asteroid released its pent up energy against the tug, littering the heavens with a shower of silver fragments, spinning and glittering in an ever widening circle.

The end must have come swiftly for the occupant, and even if he had suited up, the impact would have made sure nothing larger than a dinner plate remained intact.

Cresswell sat back in his chair and relaxed for the first time in what seemed like days. The crisis was over, he and the tug were still intact. But what to do about his visitor?

'You need do nothing. I am here should you wish to speak, or seek advice. Everything else remains the same.'

'You must be joking,' Cresswell exploded. 'it's not every day a person has someone else rattling around in his head, if that's where you are, and listening in to his every thought.'

'I'm not in your head, well not exactly. I can't help listening in to what you think, you radiate so strongly, I am sorry if I invade your idea of self, but there is nothing I can do about it.'

'No, I'm sorry,' he replied. 'I'm not thinking straight, and that's not surprising after the events of the last few hours. I mean no criticism of you, or what you are, it's just I'm feeling a little jumpy at the moment, it'll pass, I hope. Anyway, what do I call you?'

'You do not have to call me by name, I am here all the time. If you wish to say a name, you can use Vax, it is the nearest translation from my language I can make.'

'Thank you.' Cresswell was slowly getting used to the idea of an 'internal partner', and a 'tag' would help, or so he thought.

'One question which I must ask, how can you speak my language and understand my thoughts?'

'An observation ship has had your world under surveillance ever since you left your planet's surface and began exploring your other satellites, and electronic surveillance has been going on for a long time before that. We do what you would call a shift of nearly one of your earth years, and then someone else takes over. I found it interesting to learn your

language, something to pass the time. In answer to your next question, there have been a few of your tugs around recently, and I thought it best to hide in the group of asteroid fragments in which you found me. I did not realize that they were moving so violently, and the ship was trapped before I could do anything about it. The signalling equipment was smashed almost at once, and so I could not call for help.'

'Can you not call for help using my equipment?' Cresswell offered, doubting very much if it would be of sufficient power or of the right kind.

'Thank you for your offer, but we use a totally different system of communication.'

'How long can we exist together?'

'There is no limit that I know of, as long as we keep your body alive.'

He now knew that he stood a better chance of surviving the vagaries of nature and his fellow man than just about any one alive, and it gave him a new feeling of confidence. A shattered and very exhausted Cresswell said, 'I feel very tired and would like to sleep for a while, but what will you do?'

'I do not sleep as you need to, so I will keep watch over things, and wake you should there be a need. I can still be aware of my surroundings even if your body sleeps, so you may rest without fear.'

'Thanks for that. I'll park the tug in a safe orbit and get some rest, I ache all over.' With that he stabilized the craft around a large asteroid, put the fleece cover back on his sleep pod, climbed in and fell asleep.

Nature, chance, or call it what you will, has a strange way of redressing the imbalances brought about by its lesser mortals, sometimes.

The Assayers had fiddled with the computer, trying to delay Cresswell's enormous credit transfer while he had his 'accident', but the computer didn't like it, and forced the entry through anyway. Much later, when the Assayers realized something had gone horribly wrong with their scheme, they released their 'fiddle' in the hope of covering up their tracks, and the same amount was entered again, and debited to the Assayer's account.

As there were now two identical entries, the computer, in its housekeeping mode, detected this, did an electronic 'hiccup' and erased the authorization of the first entry, but leaving the transfer intact. Cresswell was now very rich.

He came out of his long and well earned sleep feeling much better, and then recalled the strange events of the last few hours before he had rested. He still found it difficult to reconcile the fact that there were now two of them, but as the other being seemed to be benign, and had indeed saved his life, although not for purely altruistic reasons, he felt safe in the knowledge that he now had a protector of considerable means, and this upped his survival rating.

What he would do when returning to the smelter station with regard to the attempted murder of his person, he wasn't sure, but he would have to face them sooner or later. Who exactly was behind the attempt? He could only guess, it might well be the Assayers or someone to do with the fund holders of the station.

He could go to one of the other stations, but felt it was a little like dealing with foreigners somehow, and if they got wind of his predicament, would no doubt take every advantage of it, and short change him as well.

He resolved to tackle that problem later, as there were more important things to do out here in the belt, not least, keeping an eye open for another attempt on his life.

He didn't think they would give up that easily, and would probably want him out of the way in case he caused trouble by reporting the murder attempt.

Yes, he would have to keep a careful watch on anything which looked a little out of the ordinary, which brought him back to his new companion.

'Vax, can you hear me?' he still spoke the words out loud from force of habit.

'I am always here, there is no need to prefix what you want to say with my name.'

'What do you think we should do now, apart from keep an eye out for further attacks?'

'Your purpose for being here remains the same, so why not look for the asteroids your people prize so much.   There is little else out here to occupy you, and in time you will need to replenish your stores, so you must have something to trade with, although it would seem that you have a large amount of trading power held on the smelter station. If you do not trade as is expected of you, suspicions may be aroused as to why you choose not to. Do not be too concerned about future attacks, between us we should be able to foil any attempts to destroy us.'

A little shiver ran down Cresswell's spine at the reference to 'us', and he thought he felt a chuckle from his companion.

A search pattern was set up on the control board, and the tug left the clump of asteroids to look for something with a high metallic content, as it was designed to do.

As he settled down to the routine of shipboard life again, he realized he was bursting with questions, and took the opportunity while the tug went about its work.

'Why are you so interested in our world when it is so far out on the rim of the galaxy?'

'We are interested in all life forms, mainly to trade with as your people do among themselves, but on a much larger scale, and chiefly for technology. In answer to your next question, we only contact stable races in person, otherwise we just observe new worlds in the hope that they may be suitable for contact in time. And no, I do not think your people will reach that stage before they destroy themselves.'

Although he agreed with the statement, he felt himself stiffen a little at the implication.

'Do not feel hurt, I merely state a fact as I see it. You are not intrinsically of this type, and I wondered why?'

'I thought you could read my every thought, and would therefore know all about me.' chided Cresswell.

'You still do not understand. I can pick up your actual thought processes, but that does not tell me why you are the way you are, only what you think at the time.'

The tug continued its search pattern, the questions and answers flowed, and what amounted to a form of friendship developed between the two. Eventually Cresswell asked,

'What is your body form like, and your world?'

'Our bodies are not too different from yours and function along the same lines, as to my home world, I'll see if I can give you a mental picture of it.'

In his mind's eye, he saw a tall well muscled figure striding about in what looked like a country scene, although the plants looked a little alien, and he hadn't seen that much unspoiled greenery for a long time.

The dwellings, he thought that's what they were, swept gracefully up to the sky, with plenty of space between them, all blending in to make a harmonious whole. The pictures were a little indistinct, but he was able to get the general idea of what Vax was endeavouring to show him.

'What do you think will happen to my world, based on the data you have obviously been collecting?'

Cresswell had to ask the question, although he felt he knew the answer deep down inside.

'Are you sure you want to know? You may not like the answer I have, as it has a very high probability of becoming fact.'

'Yes, I would. It's better to know the truth.'

'The observers stay well away from your world out here in asteroid belt, and well screened from your people, or we were until you came looking for minerals. We send small probes down to the surface to inform us of what is going on. You are only allowed to learn what others wish you to know, so you will not know of the latest developments on your world. Quite some time ago, a new kind of computer was built, using a hybridised organic material which gave it vastly superior power and speed over that which had gone before. Most manufacturing is now automated to a degree which is dangerous among people like yours, and sooner or later the machines will take over.   No, not like that!'

Again, Cresswell felt that chuckle.

'What I mean is, they will be able to repair and replicate themselves and develop without the necessity of outside information. As so many are now linked to each other, in an electronic sense, they can communicate, and no doubt will develop some form of self preservation before long, that is the danger. Your people have given too much control to machines, and just let them get on with supplying their needs with little thought of the outcome. We have come across similar situations like this before, and although these machines can not think and reason as we can, they can get a very close approximation to it.'

'You mean the machines might take over from man, and do away with him?' asked an incredulous Cresswell.

'It all depends upon how they are programmed, the more complex the computing power, the more carefully they need to be programmed. If they also have self preservation built into them, then how could you shut it off once it had been initiated, if closing down the program negates the purpose?'

'I see what you mean. I know things are a bit fraught on earth, but I don't see them getting that bad, or do you know something I don't ?'

'Greed, corruption, and general lack of ethics has turned your people into a very materialistic race, and if that gets out of hand, as it is doing, all perspective on human values will be lost, only the possession of things will matter. When this gets out of control it can lead to war, as one side tries to take from the other that which it wants, by force.'

'That's basically why I like being on my own, I have few friends, and don't trust any of 'em.'

Cresswell felt somewhat depressed after looking at the situation, which he knew existed, but didn't want to confront it to the degree he had just done.

At that moment, the object sensor bleeped its warning that something had been detected, and he left his gloomy thoughts at the prospect of locating another asteroid of ore.

As they drew nearer to the mass which had triggered the sensor, it became apparent that it wasn't going to be another giant lump of ore. Something reflected the dim sunlight, making it look a lot larger than it really was, but the mass indicator showed a surprisingly high reading.

'Could be we have a solid lump of something very heavy here, and that usually means a metal.'

He enjoyed the idea of talking to someone rather than just to himself.

The asteroid itself was only a little larger than the tug, but registered a mass of over one hundred and fifty fold that of the craft which had located it. Cresswell was mentally rubbing his hands with glee, this could fetch a small fortune if it was a rare metal.

Slowly the tug edged closer, and he got ready to leave the craft and obtain a sample for testing.

The hatch shut with a clunk, and he began the journey across the intervening space to the shiny object ahead.

Thinking of the fortune he was going to make, Cresswell fired the small holding bolt to which he would attach his secondary line, and it bounced off the surface in a shower of sparks, spinning off into space and only just missing him.

'Please take more care,' the voice in his head said.

The involuntary jump Cresswell made when the bolt flew by caused him to drift off the surface of the asteroid, and he was floating in space again, but still attached to his main line. A quick pulse on the propulsion unit brought him back to the surface as he tried in vain to find a hand hold, but the surface was too smooth and shiny.

He was slowly drifting around the curve of the asteroid when he came across an old towing bolt, firmly driven in.

Someone else had tried to bring this beauty home, and failed. But why? A very small ragged piece of tow line was still attached to the bolt, and just visible in the faint light.

Something had caused the line to break, and he had never known that to happen, so what could have caused the break, and what had happened to the former finder? Why hadn't he come back?

An uneasy feeling overcame him, and he felt he should abandon the asteroid to its fate in the belt.

'I see no reason to leave it here, I am sure we could move it somehow, and it would gain you many credits.'

'I don't like the idea of someone else trying to capture it, and failing. Something has broken the towing cable right next to the holding bolt, and I've never known that to happen. I feel there's something unknown and sinister about this lump of rock, and I don't like it.'

'You are giving way to your emotions and fears unnecessarily, it is but a piece of mineral, most likely broken off a larger piece or even a fragment of an old planet which has disintegrated. It has no life force of its own, or means of defending itself from whatever you wish to do to it.'

'All right, I'll try and uncouple the old tow line, and then see if I can attach our own line to the bolt.'

Using small bursts from his propulsion unit, he got near enough to the abandoned towing bolt to grab hold of it, and so stop himself from spinning off into space again.

'I'll put my secondary line on first.' Cresswell said. 'I want to look this thing over before we commit ourselves to anything we may not be able to get out of later.'

It wasn't easy in gloved hands to attach his own line to the abandoned bolt with its tuft of frayed cable, but he managed to do it after much cursing under his breath.

'This surface doesn't look natural somehow, it's far too smooth and glassy, although it has been made to look knobbly and natural.' He began to crawl along the surface of the asteroid, holding on to any protuberances available and using small bursts from his propulsion unit when he occasionally drifted away.

He had crawled fifteen metres or so when he reached a ridge and peered over cautiously. Before him was a gaping hole leading down into the interior of the asteroid.

'I was right,' his voice boomed out in the close confines of his helmet, 'this is not a natural object, the hole in front of me has been machined out of the body of the asteroid and leads deep inside by the look of it.'

'I know, I can see it too, don't forget.'

'What do we do now?' Cresswell asked, knowing full well what he intended to do.

'We can go in, if we are careful and the line is long enough. I do not sense any danger, as yet.'

Slowly, he eased himself over the edge of the hole, and spreading his arms out to touch the sides, was able to propel himself down into the inky depths below.

Suddenly he hit the bottom of the hole, and flexing his knees he was able to absorb what little shock there was, and so avoided bouncing back out of the hole again.

The hand lamp sent a swathe of brilliant white light sweeping around the bottom of the hole, but it wasn't the end of the tunnel. The passage in the rock turned around at ninety degrees, and carried on into the darkness.

'So far, so good.' Cresswell was enjoying the experience of exploring something so obviously alien, and intended to carry on to see what else he might find.

'Proceed with caution, if you please. I think this artifice was once part of something a lot larger, and we do not know if the structure is safe.'

'It looks solid enough to me, and there's quite a bit of line left, so I'll go on to the end, if I can reach it.'

There was no sense of up or down, only the tunnel going on into the darkness.

The asteroid seemed to be bigger on the inside than it looked from the surface, but as they hadn't been all around it, they had no idea of its length.

Suddenly the tunnel came to an end. What looked like a solid door blocked the way, and he paused before it looking for some means to affect an opening.

'There's nothing to turn or get a hold of.' a frustrated Cresswell said, disappointment clearly sounding in his voice.

'If you look at about half your height, you will see a small hole or depression, see if you can get a finger into it.'

'How come you saw it and I didn't, when we both use the same pair of eyes?' Cresswell was getting a little bit irritated at being outsmarted so frequently by his involuntary companion.

'It is a matter of interpreting the data received by the eyes for what it really is, rather than what you expect, and no, I am not what you think of as a 'smart arse', I am only doing what I am able to do to ensure the survival of us both, and your body.'

'Point taken, I'm sorry, I didn't mean to be offensive.'

Hurriedly, he managed to get a gloved finger into the depression and pushed, hoping the door would swing open and reveal something mind boggling enough to take their combined selves off the more touchy subject as to who was the brighter, but nothing happened.

'Try pulling the closure to one side, and then the other,' the voice echoed in his head.

A push to the right did nothing, but the door slid to one side effortlessly when he tried in the other direction.

Shining the light into the cavernous space beyond the doorway revealed a series of bench like objects, some of which had a strange script upon them, interspersed with coloured discs and raised portions of the surface which looked as if they were meant to be turned or pushed.

'Now ain't that something.' was all Cresswell could say as he stared in disbelief at the alien controls, but of what?

'Do not touch anything until we can decipher what the controls are for, and if there is likely to be any backlash harmful to us should we use them.'

'Don't worry, I don't want to go up in smoke having come this far, anyway, I expect it's all damaged beyond repair. As you say, it was probably part of something much larger, and without the rest of it, I doubt if it will work. That's if we can figure out what it is.'

Cresswell could feel his heart thumping inside his ribcage as he fully realized the significance of what they had found.

So far, the existence of an alien race had been only speculation, although the possibility of such was always on the cards, considering the number of suns and attendant Planets which were known to exist.

It was always understood that one day man would come up against another race, but so far there was no proof that any existed. There was now, and Cresswell could hardly wait to spread the good, or bad news, depending upon where one stood on the subject.

'I can understand your excitement about what we have found, but we must be cautious and consider the effects if we were to inform your people of this. Let us see what we have found before we make any decisions.'

Cresswell moved into the control room, holding onto the bench-like structures to prevent himself from floating around like a piece of driftwood in a lazy river.

Having reached down the side of what he thought was about the middle of the room, he paused to turn his hand light around on the rest of the cavern.

'This must have been part of something very big if the numbers of controls are anything to go by.' was the only comment he could think of.

'I have not seen anything quite like this before, so I am sure it does not belong to my race. I am not so surprised as you are to discover this device, as we have known for a long time that others exist.'

As 'they' stood there looking around at the strange alien devices around the cavern, something somewhere must have sensed their presence, as the lights slowly came on to illuminate the great room.

'There must be a power source here somewhere, and as it is still working, we must suppose that other things are also functional. Great caution must be taken with regard to trying out the controls.'

Cresswell wondered how the eyes of the alien builders worked, as the blue light was very close to ultraviolet, and was beginning to hurt his eyes.

As he went on down the side of the cavern, Cresswell became aware that his companion was taking control of his eyes to some degree, as every now and then he found them suddenly flickering to one side or the other for a second look at something, and he didn't like the sensation one bit.

'I am sorry to cause you discomfort, but I need to take in all the data I can in order to deduce the purpose for which this control system was built.'

'Oh, that's all right, help yourself, there's little I can do about it anyway.' he was still a little peeved at the thought that he was no longer in full control of his body.

By the time 'they' had been down one side of the cavern and back up the other, Cresswell was beginning to feel tired and very thirsty.

'I sense your body needs rest, or perhaps it is you who need to take a break from this place for a short while. Just relax a moment, and recall how it feels to sleep.'

Cresswell without realizing it, did just that, and drifted off into a deep slumber.

The next thing he knew was that he was snap wide awake, all feeling of tiredness gone but he still felt very thirsty.

'How long have I been asleep?   I assume that's what's happened.'

'For quite a while by the way you measure time. It was long enough for me to come to a conclusion about this room. It is the control centre of a fusion plant, probably supplying power to the rest of the construction before whatever disaster overtook the complete unit. I found an opening in the floor which led down to another level, and that was where I found what could well be a fusion generator of some kind.   I would assume

that the rest of the controls here belong to the rest of the complete unit. Only these two panels are associated with the generator itself, as the symbols on the power unit and these panels are the same.'

Cresswell watched, fascinated, as his arm seemed to adopt a life of its own and swept around to indicate the two control units in question.

'Do you think the plant would still work?' asked Cresswell with visions of taking a complete working fusion generator back to earth orbit, and rubbing a few very senior noses of the scientific council in the fact that it could be done.

'I do not know if the actual generator is still complete, although it looks as though there is no damage down there that I can see. We could try to see if we can switch it on, as I would assume that it was automatically shut down when the disaster happened.

Is it all right if I take full control of your body again? I may have to react very quickly if anything should go wrong.'

'Yes, that's fine by me, only I want to see what's happening as well.'

'You will.'

A slight feeling of being somewhere else swept over Cresswell. It was only slight, and subtle in it's effect, and he was aware that his body was now moving very purposefully under the control of something which seemed to have no hesitation of what it was about to do.

He watched as his fingers danced among the coloured discs and knobs, touching here, pressing there, until the discs one by one, lit up from within.

Although he could hear nothing, he could feel a deep vibration through his feet as they were on with the floor of the cavern, and almost at once there were a quick series of bright blue white flashes of light lancing down the tunnel they had come in by. It lit the cavern up starkly, throwing deep shadows where anything protruded from the walls, even the little knobs on the control panels cast long thin shadows across the otherwise smooth surfaces.

Almost in the same instant, and feeling a little dizzy from the speed of his body's reaction, his fingers flew across the panels again, the lights behind the coloured discs going out one by one until all was as it had been only a few moments earlier.

'It would seem that the generator is complete and working well, the bright flashes of light being due to an intense electric discharge somewhere on the outer surface where the power cables have been severed from whatever they supplied before the disaster. I thought it wise to shut the generator down before the power surge melted the surface,

and blocked our escape.'

'I can hardly believe this is happening.' Cresswell finally managed to blurt out, 'It's like a dream. We find proof of an alien race, twice over, and then find a fusion generator in working order. No one is going to believe this unless we get the generator back to earth orbit, but I'm not so sure that's a good idea, anyway, come to think of it.'

'Why not? It could earn you a vast amount of your credits which you all seem so keen to collect, and you would be held in great esteem by your fellow people.'

'That's the theory.' said Cresswell, knowing his people only too well. 'I doubt if I would last out the next twenty four hours after the generator arrived. I don't think you fully understand just what's at stake here. Vast amounts of money have been invested in fission generators, as polluting as they are, and no one is going to be very happy if I turn up with something which will replace them overnight, so to speak.

And then there is the problem of keeping the technology to myself until a deal can be struck. The only thing which is likely to be struck is me, and that now means you as well.

'Unless you can think of a way around these problems, we are stuck out here with something most civilized races would give their eye teeth for, but my lot aren't civilized, by any stretch of the imagination.'

'Surely your people would be only too pleased to have such a renewable, safe and pollution free power source, and costing so little to run?'

'Let me tell you a little story I read as a boy. Apparently there was this man who had come up with a fuel stretching system. It basically consisted of a stabilized colloidal solution of hydrogen pentoxide and petroleum spirit. As the petrol burnt, it broke down the colloidal suspension of the pentoxide, releasing oxygen. This extra oxygen then enabled the carbon-monoxide which had been generated by the petrol to burn very hotly, and the excess heat flashed the water vapour left over from the pentoxide to steam, producing even more power. In effect, this meant that you could get just about twice the amount of energy from a given amount of petroleum. The petroleum companies didn't like this idea because it meant that their sales would fall by about half, and therefore their profits.

'Never mind the benefits to the human race, that sort of thing just doesn't come into the calculation. Seventeen people either had fatal accidents or went missing before the lid was finally put on that idea.

'Years later, someone else came up with the idea, and because of the way the principle was   broadcast to all and on something they called the Internet, the companies could do nothing about it, and it went into use, and as far as I know is still in use today, in a modified form. That is the kind of thing we are up against.'

'*As I have explained before, my people are only here to observe your world and check on its progress, but it is difficult not to build up a feeling of brotherhood with your people after a time. It saddens me greatly to find that they are so retarded on a mental level to almost negate their progress.*'

'Oh, they'll make progress scientifically all right, and always have done. Whether they'll blow themselves into oblivion in the process is another matter, and by the way things are going at the moment I wouldn't be in the least bit surprised if they did.'

There was a long silence between Cresswell and his companion, as there was little else to say on the matter. But then fate took a hand, and he grabbed frantically for a hand hold on the control consul as the whole room began to slowly turn on its axis.

'What the hell's happening?' he shouted, regretting it instantly.

'*It would seem that something has caused this part of the station to rotate. I do not know why. We had better retreat to the surface to see what is doing this.*'

Getting into the power plant had been relatively easy, but getting out in a hurry seemed to take very much longer for some reason, or so it seemed to Cresswell, and he was breathing hard by the time he had regained the surface of the asteroid, as he still liked to think of it.

The light within the power plant made the blackness of space all the blacker, and the diamond brilliant pinpoint light of the stars shone all the brighter for it, as they slowly wheeled over head.

Whatever had caused the power plant to rotate, ceased to do so, and Cresswell grabbed the edge of the hole he had just emerged from to stop himself from being thrown off into space due to the momentum he had picked up from the rotating rock mass. The stars were still once more as he and his companion surveyed the scene, trying to make some sense of what had just happened.

'*I think we should return to the safety of your vessel and see what happens next. That rotation must have had a purpose behind it, and other things may well happen.*'

'I certainly agree with that.' Cresswell replied, and hauled himself hand over hand back to the anchor bolt to which he had affixed his secondary line.

His fingers seemed thick and stiff as he desperately tried to untie the line before some other unexpected event took place, and upon release, the line automatically rewound itself back into its holder.

Attaching the main ship's line to his belt, he gave it a somewhat indecent tug, and accelerated away from the power plant, the hull of his own ship looming up far quicker than he would have liked. And then he realized why. The rotation of the power plant had wound a portion of the cable around the rocky surface, and imparted a degree of motion to the ship. It was sheer luck that the rotation had been slow and the cable hadn't snapped under the strain.

A quick blast on the propulsion unit slowed him down, and a not too undignified entry into the hatch found him breathing hard and sweating profusely.

Regaining the sanctity of the main cabin, he divested himself of the space suit, took a long pull on the drink dispenser and sat down with a deep sigh.

'I think you should check the position of your ship with regard to the power plant. It may still be on an approach course due to the tug on the cable.'

Cresswell fairly hurled himself across the tiny room to the main control panel and switched on the forward viewer all in one fluid motion.

The ship was definitely moving towards the asteroid. A quick stab on the forward thruster control stopped the ship and rammed him hard up against the control panel, knocking the breath out of him.

'Thanks Vax,' he finally gasped, 'that was a close one. I don't think we would have hit head on, but even a glancing blow would have caused considerable damage. I think we'll pull away a little more to see what else may occur. As you said earlier, something may well happen.'

Disconnecting the towing cable, the tug was slowly eased away from the now stationary power plant to what they considered to be a safe distance, and he was able to collect his thoughts together for the first time in many hours.

As he relaxed in his chair, his eyes slowly began to close, and a warm feeling of contentment swept over him to be displaced by the sensation of his eyes being forced open and the harsh light of the cabin flooding in.

'I think you should look at the top right corner of the screen. Something is moving and obscuring the stars as it does so.'

Something was on the move, and it was big by any standards.

Cresswell and his companion watched fascinated, as the huge bulk of something as black as space itself slowly drifted towards the power plant.

When they thought it would hit the power plant 'asteroid' with a shattering impact, it decelerated to a barely discernible movement, and gently edged into contact.

'It would seem that something we did on the power plant has activated a response in the plant and the new mass which has just moved into contact with it. There may be other pieces of the whole unit around, and we should be aware that we may be in their way, should they also be attracted to the plant. I would think there must be some mechanism on board these pieces, which when triggered, have the effect of bringing them all together again.

'Surely that would imply there is some living thing or entity on board the pieces. How else could they sense each other's presence, and then manoeuvre into position?

'I do not think anything is alive, in the sense we use the term, as all the breathable atmosphere drained out into space when the complete unit was broken up. But consider, it is an alien device the like of which I have no knowledge, and therefore could contain a controlling mechanism of a type unknown to either of us.'

'I think we had better put a little more space between us, just in case there are other pieces moving around.'

'That would be wise. I think there is something else about to join the other two pieces, look at the top of the screen.'

The stars were being blanked out again as another mass slowly drifted down towards the 'asteroid', and he eased the little tug back still further, keeping a watchful eye on the other screens in case he was caught from behind.

Over the course of the next few hours several more pieces of varying sizes joined the power plant, wriggling into position like a living organism and sending a cold shiver down the spine of an incredulous Cresswell.

'I just can't believe this is happening.' he gasped as last, with a nervous laugh. 'Are you sure this isn't some sort of hallucination?'

'My friend, when you are confronted with something you can not understand, you must discard all the preconceived ideas you may hold, and just observe. From what you see, you can then extrapolate further data, and so come to some understanding of the whole. There are many more things in the limitless bounds of space that you or I have never

dreamed of, let alone seen. Let us watch the proceedings from a safe distance for a little longer, and then we may have more data upon which to reach an understanding of what we see.'

'Can't argue with that, Vax. Anyway, I don't feel like hitching my tow line to that thing out there any more. It's just as likely to take us for a ride.'

The hours dragged on, and after several breaks for refreshment and short fitful sleep periods with one eye held partly open by his companion, a rather worn and weary Cresswell concluded that nothing else much was going to happen to the alien mass just ahead of them.

All motion of the moving pieces had ceased some time ago, and no other parts of the alien artefact had joined the collection for several hours.

'What do we do now?' asked Cresswell, who after the excitement of recent past events was feeling somewhat dejected at the lack of action.

'I think we should wait a little longer, just in case there are a few more scattered pieces which have not reached their destination. Then it is up to you what we do. I would suggest that we leave well alone for the time being, as we do not know what purpose the whole unit was intended for. We could look for your minerals and come back at a later time to see what has transpired, or we could just stay here and observe for a while longer.'

Just then, a tiny pin prick of brilliant white light could be seen tracing a path across the now enormous collection of rock like pieces of the alien conglomeration.

'Good god, don't say the damn thing is trying to weld itself together.'

'It would seem that something of that nature is taking place, and I would suppose there must be some sort of self repairing mechanism involved. This is very interesting indeed. I have known of something similar, but on a much smaller and simpler scale. I think we should watch proceedings a little longer, and see what happens when the repair event concludes.'

There were now several fiery traces moving about on the mass ahead of them, weaving about like living entities intent on some unfathomable purpose, the like of which they could only guess at.

'I think we should move a little further away from the mass for while so that you can get a proper rest, for I sense that you are very tired and we shall need all our senses about us if you do what I think you intend. Not that I agree with that intention fully, but I too am intrigued by what

we have seen.'

'You are of course, right, as always.' There was a little chuckle in Cresswell's voice as he went to the controls and moved the tug several kilometres away from the alien ship.

Switching on all the motion detector devices and other sensors which he thought should give them ample warning of any impending action on the part of the alien ship, he set his chair to the reclining position, and lay back to take a well earned rest.

'I will help you into a deep and restful sleep, if you will allow me to, and I will keep watch for any warnings your detection devices may give. Rest assured, you will be quite safe, for I too am involved in this matter.'

'Thanks Vax, I could do with a good long sleep, I must admit.' And with that Cresswell closed his eyes and fell swiftly into what an observer could only conclude was a deep coma.

The stars turned in their heavenly dance about the tug, and the robot welders finished their scurrying manoeuvres on the mass of rocks which was the alien ship, bringing the collection of parts to an almost complete whole. Unfortunately, a few pieces were still missing, being shattered beyond all hope of recovery, and speeding on their way out of the solar system by the colossal force which had destroyed the ship in the first place.

Cresswell came out of his long and deep sleep feeling totally refreshed, both mentally and physically.

'Thanks for that, Vax. I feel reborn, and very hungry.'

'I do not understand 'reborn', please explain.'

'What I mean is, I feel new, er, not tired. Like a piece of machinery that hasn't been used yet.'

'Oh, I understand now. Yes, you will need refreshment, you have been asleep for some considerable time. There has been no noticeable action occurring on the alien ship that I could see, so I suppose that all the repair work that is possible has been done, and the ship has gone into what you would refer to as a 'waiting mode'. I suppose you now want to return to the alien ship to see what has happened?'

'You know damn well I do. I also know that you could stop me if you chose to. How dangerous do you think it would be to take a quick look close up to it?'

'If we proceed with all possible caution, and are ready to retreat swiftly, I think the dangers are minimized, but not altogether removed. We do not know if the ship has any defence systems, so a controlled approach is called for.'

Slowly the little tug drew nearer to the dwarfing alien conglomeration of what looked like rocks, but there was no reaction from the mass which they could discern.

'What now?' asked Cresswell, uncertain as to the next safe move, 'we are within line anchoring distance, but I don't like the idea of tying the tug to that lump of rock in case it decides to move off, and us with it.'

'Wisely so. I suggest we leave the tug a safe distance from it, and go in with your suit propulsion unit. An extra oxygen supply would be a good idea, just in case we are unexpectedly detained.'

He was beginning to feel a little nervous about the whole idea and tried to hide it, but then realized that his companion would have picked it up anyway, and so gave up any pretence of overt bravery.

Parking the tug in stationary orbit around the alien mass, he left the safety of the little ship and began the journey across the dark intervening space to the forbidding black mass of the camouflaged asteroid.

As he drew nearer, he realized just how big the alien structure was, blotting out a large area of the star field.

More by luck than judgement, Cresswell found the old anchoring bolt, and attached his line to it as before.

'Shall we go in at the hole we found before, or look for another one somewhere else?'

'I think we should go for the first one, we at least know we can get down it, and no harm came to us last time.'

Crawling over the surface in what he thought was the correct direction, Cresswell came across the first of the joints welded by the robots.

'Apart from the extra shine where the seams were molten, you would never know they had done it,' commented Cresswell, 'that's some technology they have, we couldn't do that.'

As there was no comment from his companion, he crawled on, using the propulsion unit every now and again to take him down to the surface when he got too energetic and floated away.

'This is the ridge where we found the hole last time, but the space is now occupied by that huge lump of rock, and there's no sign of the entrance hole.'

'Go around the other side of it. It might just be that the rock is a concealment for the entrance way.'

Cresswell didn't have much hope of that being so, as the new lump of rock filled the little valley beyond the ridge right across to the other side, where it continued as a relatively flat surface.

Doing as his companion suggested, as there seemed little alternative, he made his way hand over hand across the rocky surface until he reached the far side of what had been the valley.

'It looks as if the robots have filled in all the spaces between the new rock and the place we went in last time.'

'Go on a little further, the hole we went in must connect up with something, but it may not be obvious.'

Cresswell crawled on, and then he saw the opening. It was cleverly disguised under a small overhang of the new rock. Shining his hand lamp into the opening he could see in for about five metres, the rest of the tunnel being blocked by what looked like a solid rock surface.

Do we go in?' he asked, rather hoping for a negative answer.

'I think it should be safe, this whole artefact is purely mechanical in nature so we are unlikely to be attacked by anyone, which I sense is your worst fear.'

He remembered the little welding robots, and wasn't too sure if mechanical was quite the right word.

Gripping the edge of the entrance, Cresswell swung his body into the short tunnel and stretched his arms apart to get a purchase on the walls, enabling him to propel himself along until he reached the solid looking wall of stone barring his way.

'Now what? There's no knob, latch, hole or anything else to open the door with, that's if it's a door in the first place.'

'Patience, my friend. Let us use a little reason here. There is an opening. It looks as if it leads to a way inside the rock. Why else would it be there? There is no other reason, therefore there must be a way in. There is no sign of an opening tool or handle, so therefore it must open by sensing someone or something. It is not likely to be one of your card readers, as a gloved hand in space would be hard put to use one. Move a little closer, touch the stone, try anything which comes to mind.'

Cresswell took a step closer, pushing on the side walls to do so. He touched the end blockage, hit it with his clenched gloved hand, and wished he hadn't been so enthusiastic in delivering the blow, and then stepped back in frustration.

The stone slid back revealing a dimly lit passage with a blocked end.

Cresswell just stood there, not really wanting to go in now that they had got this far. There was too much of the unknown about this whole affair, and he felt uneasy about presenting his body to the alien space ship in case it didn't like him.

Before he could stop himself, he had taken a step into the tunnel, and the stone slab slid across the entrance behind him, blocking their escape.

'Sorry to have taken control just then, but we needed to move in quickly or the doorway would have sensed something was wrong and may not have opened again to us.'

'That's fine, but we are now trapped in the passageway.' replied Cresswell, a nervous edge to his voice.

'Go up to the next stone block, this may be an airlock.'

Cresswell did as he was bid, and the solid stone wall in front of him slid to one side as the other one had done, revealing the dimly lit tunnel extending into the distance, until the pale light would allow no more detail to be seen.

'As there was no rush of atmosphere when the doors opened, we can safely assume that the craft is not sealed and therefore there can be no life forms on board, or at least not live ones. I would think that when disaster struck this vessel it was broken apart instantly, and everything which was not secured in a fixed position, including the crew, would have been sucked out into space. I do not think we have anything to fear, apart from fear itself. Let us go on down the passage to the control room and see what else we can find since the reconstruction.'

Cresswell felt a little better having got the situation into perspective, and pushed against the glass smooth walls to propel himself along to the end of the tunnel.

As he entered the control room he noticed there was a change about the place. For one thing there was a sense of gravity, as his body drifted down to what he assumed to be floor level, and if he moved very gently, he could almost walk in a normal manner.

Many of the coloured discs were now lit up from within and a gentle low vibration could be felt through his feet, but there was no sound as the vacuum of space still pervaded the whole craft, and sound needed some sort of atmosphere to travel through.

'The power plant seems to be working, and as there were no sparks on the outside of the craft, the lines must have been connected up to whatever they were intended to supply. I think we should trace them, as that would give us an idea of what duties this craft was intended to perform. Let us look for another doorway which might lead us to a different section of the craft.'

Cresswell found the hole in the floor which led down to the actual power plant itself, but thought that the doorway, if it existed, would most likely be in the control room.

He walked the length of the room, studying each of the consoles in turn to see if he could make sense of what they were intended to do, but the symbols meant nothing to him.

It was on his second time around that he found the doorway. It was almost invisible in the pale light of the room, just a faint outline in the otherwise smooth surface.

'Looks like we've found it.' he announced triumphantly, and moved as close to the surface as he could without falling over backwards. Nothing happened.

'Step back, as you did before. For some reason, which I have not yet discovered, the doorways need you to do that.'

Cresswell stepped back as instructed, and the wall obligingly slid back to reveal another tunnel leading off into the distance.

'Here we go.' said Cresswell, as he stepped into the new tunnel, and gave an involuntary jump as the slab of rock-like substance slammed to cover the opening behind him.

The light seemed to come out of the very substance of the walls forming the tunnel, and bathed the area in a soft and gentle glow, a little towards the blue end of the spectrum, but giving clear detail to all around him.

He had been travelling for some minutes when he stopped suddenly. Just ahead there was a hole in the top of the passageway and the stars could be seen shining beyond.

'This must be a section where there is a missing piece of the structure, and the welding robots were unable to bridge the gap. The hole is big enough for you to crawl through should we become trapped, so it is safe to carry on.'

He carefully checked to see if he could get out through the hole in the roof of the tunnel, and having satisfied himself that he could, walked on down the passageway.

The gravity seemed to increase a little as he walked on, and he thought that indicated he was going deeper into the mass of the craft, and therefore possibly to other rooms.

Rounding a bend, the passageway came to an abrupt end. In front of the solid wall before him Cresswell saw a gaping hole, the same size as the tunnel and going vertically downwards.

'I'm not going to jump down there, god knows how deep it is, or what's at the bottom.'

'It is not necessarily down or up, but just part of the tunnel complex. The gravity is very low, so you should not gain a great deal of velocity even if it is in a relatively downward direction. If you step into the hole and spread your arms out to touch the sides, you should be able to control your descent, if you feel uncertain of proceeding.'

Drawing a deep breath, Cresswell stepped over the hole, spread his arms, and slowly drifted downwards.

The tunnel must have had a bend or twist in it, which he hadn't noticed, as before long Cresswell found himself lying on his side on the tunnel floor slowly sliding along, coming to a halt just before he reached another hole.

Peering over the edge, he let out an exclamation of surprise. Below him was a large room, brightly lit compared to the tunnels, and as far as his vision extended, adorned with a collection of consoles similar to those he had seen earlier.

'We've found something here, shall I jump down?'

'You will have to if you want to enter the room.'

Cresswell eased himself over the edge of the hole, holding on with one hand while he made sure he wouldn't land on top of anything below, and then let go to drift slowly downwards.

Landing gently on his feet in the middle of the room, he looked around for any possible threat to his being there, but all he could see were the consoles with their colourfully lit discs and a large screen covering the end wall.

'What do you suppose this room is all about then?'

'It is difficult to say without a survey of the controls. Move among them and I will see if any are similar to those we saw in the power control room.'

Cresswell slowly walked around the consoles lining the walls, but to him they meant nothing apart from the colourful display of lights.

'Do not touch anything yet, we do not know what these controls do or what their purpose is.'

'Don't worry, I'm not in the habit of taking chances like that Vax, anyway, I don't suppose they would blow the place up as it would defeat the purpose of the craft being here in the first place.'

He could hardly have missed it, as it covered the entire end of the room, and was about to vocalize a sarcastic comment to that effect when he was interrupted.

'There is a disc on the middle console with the same shape and rim pattern as the actual screen. I would think that touching it might turn *it on.'*

Cresswell moved over to the console in question, and noticed the similarity of the symbol. He reached out to touch the disc, hesitated a moment, and found his hand moving to complete the move of its own volition.

He nearly fell over backwards in an act of self preservation as the end wall suddenly came to life in a blaze of light. It was if the wall had disappeared completely, and they were looking out into the endless depths of space.

'My god, what a sight, it's even better than actually being out there.'

'That is because of the contrast of being enclosed by these walls around us. It is only a screen, go forward and touch it to be sure. I have calculated that we must be somewhere in the middle of the craft, so it can not be real.'

He walked forward, still not entirely convinced that it wasn't real, and holding on to the last console in the line, reached forward to touch what looked like empty space, and found something quite solid but invisible.

'This place is certainly full of surprises.'

'In a totally alien environment, you should expect surprises, and as you say, there are likely to be many more. But caution is to be maintained if we are to come to no harm, the unexpected is all around us.'

Cresswell just stood there, mesmerized by the sheer beauty of the scene, until an impatient companion reminded him that there were other things to find out about the alien craft.

Three:
Time Slip

'I HAVE A *feeling that we are intended to explore this craft, as a test of our intelligence and reasoning powers. Therefore, still being very cautious, I think we should try to activate as many of the controls as we can, but only after we have reasoned out what they might be for.'*

'That sounds like a good idea, but the symbols are meaningless to me and you said that you hadn't come across anything like this before, so how can we work out what does what?'

'*We have done quite well so far, and come to no harm. I do not think this craft is intended to cause us harm or it would have done so long ago. Let us explore as much of this room as possible, and see what we can decipher from the symbols and any other marking there may be.*'

Cresswell walked the length of the room slowly, glancing at all the control units as he passed and hoping that Vax would do the job of working out what they were for, as he couldn't make any sense of them and saw no relation between the coloured discs and the other devices dotted around the floor of the room.

Reaching the far end wall, he did notice a square marked out on the floor, about a metre across and clearly defined.

'What do you think that's for?' he asked, seeing no obvious reason for it being there.

'*I think we should stand on it, and see if something happens. There do not seem to be any controls related to it as far as I can see.*'

Cresswell bent down to look a little more closely at the line defining the square, and decided that the centre section looked a little different to the surrounding floor, and said so to Vax.

'*I think it is safe to stand on, so let us do that.*'

He thought he detected a slight touch of impatience in Vax's reply, and stepped onto the square.

For a moment nothing happened, but just as Cresswell was about to step back onto the safety of the main floor there was a soft sigh, felt through his feet rather than heard, and the square he was standing on slowly descended into a shaft, the room above disappearing from view.

'Now what have we got ourselves into?' demanded a slightly unnerved Cresswell.

'*You are perhaps a little too cautious. It would seem this device is a means of travelling from one level to another, and that is what we are doing.'*

The lift platform eventually broke into the space below and descended to floor level, Cresswell stepping off it as quickly as he could without making it too obvious that he still felt uneasy about the whole thing.

The space into which they had descended was more like a long tunnel than the room above, and the centre section, running into the far distance, was taken up by what looked like a half buried massive tube.

Spaced along its length at six metre intervals were a series of annular rings, also half buried, and it was to these that Cresswell felt attracted.

They appeared to be made of a glass-like substance and possibly hollow, although he couldn't be sure of their internal structure.

Before he could stop himself, he had stepped forward and his hand reached out to stroke the first of the rings. A faint glow of pale blue light followed his hand as it caressed the curved surface of the accelerator ring, and then the glow built up until it was a blaze of pure energy.

'I think you should treat all the rings in the same manner, it would seem that it is intended that they be turned on by your touch.'

'There's a hell of a lot of 'em.' replied Cresswell, looking down the tunnel to where the tube like structure seemed to merge into the tunnel walls in the far distance. There was no reply from Vax.

Cresswell had to admit to himself, and possibly Vax as well, that stroking the rings gave him a strange but pleasant sensation, and apart from the formidable thought that all the rings had to be stroked, he didn't mind doing it.

On the tenth ring, the device took control away from Cresswell. The next ring in the sequence having anticipated his touch, obligingly lit up of its own accord, and the ripple effect raced on down the tunnel until all the rings blazed out their dazzling blue light and Cresswell had to shield his eyes from the glare.

A panel on the tunnel wall suddenly came to life, a series of flashing coloured lights rippled on and off in sequence creating an almost hypnotic effect for Cresswell, who had to tear his gaze away from it with some effort.

As soon as he had averted his gaze, the lights went out, the panel returning to its normal dull colour, blending in with the tunnel wall on which it was mounted.

'What was that all about?'

'I think you have just been tested for strength of will, or something like that. So far we seem to have done everything expected of us, so perhaps we had better return to the room above as that seems to be the main control room. Also, the light level in here is still increasing, and it will soon be strong enough to cause you pain and possibly radiation burns.'

Cresswell hadn't realized just how far down the tunnel he had walked while stroking the glass-like rings on the tube structure, and felt a little tinge of fear as he failed to recognize the point at which they had entered the tunnel.

Quickening his pace as best he could in the very low gravity, he walked right past the lift platform they had used earlier without seeing it. The vibration which he could feel through his feet was changing in tone, while the increasing blaze of light from the rings was adding to his confusion and a rising level of panic.

'We have gone along the tunnel a little too far, we must have missed the lift platform somehow. We will have to go back to the last ring you touched opposite the wall panel.'

Cresswell turned a little too quickly and his forward momentum nearly caused him to topple over as he desperately tried to regain his balance.

'How come you didn't see the damned platform when we went past it?' a somewhat irritated Cresswell asked.

'Your eyes may not have been looking in that direction when we went by.'

Search as they might, the platform remained stubbornly hidden from view, and a degree of panic set in again as far as he was concerned.

Finding the panel with the now non functioning indicators was their first step to re-orientate themselves, and that proved difficult enough.

'You will have to count back ten rings, shielding your eyes with your hands and viewing them between the gaps in your fingers.'

He felt a degree of calmness returning when he realized that Vax had the situation under control once more, and set about doing as he was bid.

On reaching the tenth ring in the sequence, Cresswell turned through ninety degrees and before him was the lift platform. A sigh of relief whistled around his helmet as he stepped onto the barely visible slab, but nothing happened.

'Now what do we do?' he asked, frustration sounding in his voice once again.

'*I do not know, I would have thought it would go up automatically as we have done what was required of us. Maybe there is something else we must do first.*'

'Well, I'm not getting off this bloody platform to look for clues, that's for sure.'

Cresswell looked all around him for some sort of control device for the platform, but there was nothing, just the bare tunnel wall and an ever increasing blaze of light which he could almost feel pushing against him.

'Come on Vax, there must be something you can do. If we don't go up soon we'll be cooked to a frazzle.'

'*Let me use your eyes again, I will try not to deform them too much.*'

Having little option, Cresswell agreed, and the pain began as Vax took hold of the eye muscles and exerted his control.

Cresswell felt his eyes almost snap back into shape as Vax let go of the muscles, and he longed to rub them.

'*I can just make out eight very faint depressions in a line on the tunnel wall, there is nothing else within reach of the platform, so that must be the device for moving it. Let me guide your fingers into them.*'

Cresswell was almost past caring and nodded his agreement. His arms shot out, his fingers splayed into a fan shape and then jammed themselves hard into the surface of the wall. The lift rose quickly up into the shaft above and they were in pitch darkness until it reached the room above.

He leapt off the lift platform with indecent haste and went sprawling against the wall, cursing under his breath.

'Well, we're back in one piece, just about.'

Turning back towards the centre of the room, Cresswell was halted in his tracks by the sudden appearance of something in the middle of the space between the line of consuls.

'Where did that come from? It wasn't there earlier, there was nothing there, just bare floor!'

Slowly he approached the block of scintillating black material which seemed to have extruded itself from the floor of the room, and stopped a metre away from it.

'*Look carefully at it. It is shaped like a sitting device, similar to the one you use in the tug, and it even has a recess in the back support to accommodate your breathing pack. Somehow, something in here has measured your body and constructed this sitting device for your comfort. I think you are meant to use it. Maybe something wishes you to be comfortable while the next event unfolds.'*

'And just what do you think that might be?' asked a rather nervous Cresswell.

'I do not know. It might be that you are to watch something on the screen, for the device is pointing in that direction, or maybe something sensed that you required a sitting device, and has supplied one.'

'I don't want one, I just want to collect as much data as I can about this place and then get the hell back to my ship.'

'I think you should sit in it, and see what happens next.'

Reluctantly, Cresswell eased himself into the chair-like object and leaned back, facing the huge viewing screen.

Out of the corner of his eye, he could see several of the consoles coloured light discs flashing on and off, as if something was working the controls from within, and the hardly noticeable vibration which he had felt through his feet, suddenly changed. The change was only very slight, but to his heightened senses, it was apparent.

'I don't like this.' he said, and tried to get up.

It wasn't that anything held him down, it was just that his muscles didn't work, and he remained seated despite all efforts to rise.

'Hey, get me out of this thing Vax, I've got a nasty feeling something unpleasant is going to happen.'

'I can not. Your muscles do not respond to my override. I do not think we are in any danger. If the craft meant us any harm, it could have done so long before this. Just sit there, and see what happens.'

It wasn't long before it did.

Cresswell's stomach churned as the star field in the viewing screen suddenly whirled through two hundred degrees, and the stars began to race across the screen at an ever increasing velocity until they were represented by a series of white streaks, and then blinked out of existence, leaving the screen a jet black void.

'I would think that we are moving to a new location in space, and at a velocity which I find hard to ascertain. It must be well above the speed of light, as the stars are no longer visible. This represents a technology more advanced than that which my people have.'

'That's a comforting thought, especially as we have no control over where we are going or how to get back again.'

'I am still of the opinion that no harm will come to us. Just be patient and we will see what the craft intends for us.'

Time as such, ceased to exist for the alien craft and its occupant.

Cocooned in the tunnel of the alien warp drive, it sped across the galaxy and out into the far reaches of space, invisibly passing many more star clusters as it twisted the very fabric of time and space itself.

Faint flickers of light began to show on the screen, and slowly but surely the stars returned to view, first as streaks and then as moving points of light to eventually remain as still and brilliant as they had before.

'I do not recognize the star pattern, it is like nothing I have ever seen before,' the voice echoed in Cresswell's head as he tried to come to terms with what had just happened.

'You seem to be taking it all very calmly. Do you realize what has happened? We have been swept across half the universe and dumped in a totally strange galaxy, and no hope of returning to our own.' Cresswell was beginning to feel the first sensations of real panic.

'I understand what you are saying, but I still maintain that whatever has brought us here, means us no harm.'

The light from the closely packed star field lit the room up brightly, overriding the soft glow of the walls and adding a chill harshness to the surroundings.

'We must be in or near the centre of a galaxy for this density of stars to surround us, unlike where we came from, which was on the outer edge of a big system. This would account for the extra light, and look up there, top right of the screen, a super nova. I have never been so close to one before.'

Frightened as he was, he had to admire the sheer beauty of the scene, the many coloured stars twinkling against a vast gas cloud of new stars forming, a super nova in the full bloom of it's fiery death knell and just ahead of them, a velvet black space where nothing could be seen.

'What is that empty space just ahead? asked Cresswell, curiosity having got the better of his frightened condition.

'I am not sure, but it looks like what you refer to as a black hole in space. A massive star must have collapsed, the very atomic structure of its atoms falling in on themselves to form a small but extremely dense mass from which no light can escape. That is why we can see nothing except the area where the starlight itself is bent inwards by the massive gravitational forces of the collapsed star, and is absorbed into the mass, blanking out that which is behind it.'

'Thanks for that, but what do we do now? asked Cresswell.

'As before, we wait for whatever is scheduled to happen, I do not think it will be a long wait.'

He tried once more to rise from his stone like chair, but his muscles wouldn't respond. Once again the coloured discs began to flicker on the consoles, as some alien message triggered them into life.

A tiredness overcame him, and his eyelids felt like lumps of lead. Try as he might, they wouldn't stay open, and then he was asleep.

The dreams came quickly. He was a little boy again, rocketing down in the express lift from his high rise apartment to the pathetic little patch of dried up brown grass which represented the play area.

'Why is there no grass like that in the history discs.' he had asked his mother, but the answer was as unsatisfactory as the brown grass itself.

He recalled the pictures of wide open rolling plains and the distant hills, of strange animals roaming about in great spaces, of brilliant sunshine on sparkling water, but these were all from viewing screens, and belonged to a far distant age.

College was more fun, finding out about things, and then that was spoilt by finding out about the people there.

He had tried many jobs before he found the respite he sought from the general mayhem going on around him.

Cresswell didn't mind the stress and strain of work, he found that stimulating, it was the corruption, greed and general deceit which wore him down, and so he eventually found his niche in space.

It was lonely, but he could be himself. He didn't have to alter his values to fit in with anyone else's idea of what was right, and he was amassing a goodly amount of credits for his old age.

Perhaps he could buy that little patch of green grass and clear blue water one day. Somehow though, it didn't seem likely in reality.

His eyes opened to let in the harsh light of the teeming star clusters ahead of him, and his dreams were over.

'Have I missed anything.' he asked. 'Fancy falling asleep at a time like this.'

'I think we have, for want of a more precise expression, been scanned by something. I too felt sleepy and dreamed of my youth back home, did you dream?'

'Yes, it seemed to go on for ages, and I had no control over it. All my life seemed to flash by, my feeling and desires, everything. I feel I've been stripped naked, questioned, poked and prodded, mentally, and I now feel totally washed out.'

'I wonder what the entity who did this, made of the findings. If it looked at both our lives, and I would assume that it did, it must be very mystified as to what we are and where we came from. Our two worlds

are so very different as are our people. It must have caused a good deal of confusion.'

There was a touch of mischievous joy in his companion's voice, and Cresswell then saw the funny side of it, and laughed for the first time since leaving the smelter station so long ago.

Yet another attempt at leaving his chair proved futile, and he resigned himself to the fact that he would be released as and when 'it' whoever 'it' was, deemed it appropriate to do so.

The lights on the coloured discs began their merry dance again, and Cresswell looked on wondering what would happen next.

Once again, came the mind wrenching feeling as the alien ship suddenly turned by one hundred and eighty degrees, the stars swirled on the screen and turned into white streaks to finally wink out of existence once more as the ships incredible momentum surpassed the speed of light.

How long they travelled, they had no way of knowing, as time for them stood still, but the distance was vast by any means of measurement.

Faint streaks of light began to light the huge screen, and then the stars were back, and in the old easily recognized familiar pattern once more.

'It looks as if we're back home again.' a very relieved Cresswell finally managed to get out as he rose from his chair and stretched very stiff limbs.

'You maybe, but I am far from mine.'

'Sorry Vax, It was thoughtless to have said such a thing. I just felt so relieved to be back in familiar surroundings, with all their faults.'

The lights on the consoles went out one by one, the screen returned to its former blank state and the chair had mysteriously disappeared back into the floor while no one was looking.

'I think that is a signal for us to leave, as the whole system is beginning to shut down.'

'I would like to have a good look around first, there maybe something of use we could glean from this ship.'

'I doubt very much if we will be allowed to do very much exploring, especially of their technology, I think we should leave while we have the chance.'

It was at this point that the light from the walls began to fade, and Cresswell did his best in the low gravity to hurry over to the hole in the ceiling of the room from which he had dropped down so long ago.

Lining himself up with the tunnel entrance, he bent his knees and pushed off to float upwards through the hole and bang his head on the roof of the tunnel.

Quickly he grabbed the edge of the hole to stop himself from falling backwards, turned, rose to his feet and began the long walk back to the control room of the power plant.

'Notice how the light in the walls fades out as we progress, I think that is good evidence of the fact that we are required to leave.'

Cresswell didn't say anything, but he felt a little angry that they were not allowed to learn something of the alien technology in exchange for what they had been put through.

There was little use in pushing the point, as he realized that they could do nothing about it anyway. If the aliens wanted them out, then they would do it, one way or another, and Cresswell didn't want to hang around to see how they did it in case it had an element of terminality about it.

He eventually reached the control room, and he wondered if they had taken another route back. Hastily scrambling out of the air lock and onto the surface of the vessel, he looked around for his tug, and then his worst fear was realized as it was nowhere in sight.

His heartbeat raced up to an almost dangerous level before his companion took a hand, and brought it down again to a more sustainable level.

'Sorry to take over again, but I think you needed that intercession.'

'Damn right I did. But what are we going to do now? The tug should be visible from here, and it isn't. Without it I, I mean we, are dead as soon as the air unit packs up, and that can't be too far into the future.'

'Go back to the anchor point, maybe we can see it from there.'

His progress was painfully slow as Cresswell crawled hand over hand, trying not to launch himself into space, and so necessitate using the propulsion unit to regain the rocky surface. Every bit of fuel would be needed later, if the tug could be found.

Gaining the anchor point, he looked in all directions, but there was no sign of the tug, which should have shown up as a bright point from the reflected sunlight.

'I can't see it. Can you?' fear was welling up in Cresswell's throat like a scalding hot liquid, and his heart began to race again.

As he passed into unconsciousness, he had the foresight to grab hold of the anchor point, and Vax increased the grip as he slipped into oblivion.

'*Wake up, wake up,*' the words thundered around in his head, but he didn't want to, as it would mean confronting a spaceman's worse nightmare.

Slowly he came round, his hand aching from the force with which it had gripped the anchor point, and he released the grip a little.

'*Stand up and hook your foot around the anchor, and I will try to scan the area for the tug.*'

Cresswell did as he was bid, as he had no other solution to the desperate situation they were in, and then his eyes began to hurt as his companion began to take control of the muscles, and force his eyes into a shape they were not designed for.

'*I think I can see the tug, but it is a very long way away. We may not have enough fuel in your propulsion unit to reach it, so pick up the extra air tank you brought, it may come in useful.*'

Cresswell looked around for the spare tank he had brought, and found it lodged in a little ridge of rock a few metres away from the anchor point.

'*You will not be able to see the tug yet, so I will have to guide you in the correct direction.*'

Cresswell just grunted in reply, thought better of it, and replied properly,

'All right Vax, I'm in your hands now, I'll do whatever you say, but I'm damned if I can see anything remotely resembling the tug. It's just the awful feeling that I'm about to push off into space with nothing to aim for, just emptiness.'

'*I understand how you feel, do not forget that your fears wash over me too, but if I am to survive, I must make sure that you do as well.*'

Under his companion's direction, he positioned himself facing out into deep space, bent his knees, and pushed off. The fear still bit into his very being, but he was now committed.

Slowly the asteroid fell behind him, and he was alone out among the stars, a drifting blob of humanity clad in a space suit with a diminishing air supply, and nothing in sight to offer any comfort.

'*You are doing well, let me take your eyes again so that I can confirm we are still on our required course.*'

That awful searing pain as his eyeballs were twisted made him feel that it was all too much, but he had little choice other than to go along with what his companion wished.

'*Let me take control of the propulsion unit, it will be more efficient for me to do the course correction than to try and explain it to you.*'

Cresswell found his hands moving under their own volition, and a tiny puff of vapour from the unit turned him slightly to one side.

There was nothing to see except the distant stars, the alien asteroid having long since become a mere pinpoint of light far behind him.

Several more course corrections followed, Cresswell long since having resigned himself to whatever the fates had in store for him. His eyes hurt beyond belief from the repeated reshaping each time a course correction was done, and to top it all the first warning sound from his air supply brought him wide awake again.

'*How much time do you have before the air runs out?*' asked his companion.

'I don't know, it's not happened before, I think there are several warnings before things get desperate.' 'Desperate? How much more desperate can things get?' he asked himself.

'*We are doing well, I can see the tug clearly now, let me turn your head and you may be able to see it too.*'

Cresswell strained his painful eyes, but could see nothing except the stars.

The next course correction used up the last of the pro-propulsion units fuel supply, and a new desperation overcame him.

'*We can use the spare air tank to propel us along, as it is under pressure.*'

'Sure it's under pressure, but it mainly contains chemicals to recycle the oxygen, I don't think there's much actual gas in it. But then again, I'm not sure, I've never had the occasion to take one apart.'

'*Look again, surely you can see it now,*' and Cresswell felt his head being wrenched around to a most unnatural angle, but he didn't mind, the silver shape of the old tug could now be clearly seen even with his eyes.

'*We are directly in line with it. Only a little correction will be needed as we approach and have to lose velocity. Is it all right if I take over at the last moment to do the final approach?*'

'Yes, of course it is, just get us there in one piece. I don't care what you do as long as I can get on board again in one piece.'

A few moments later he felt his body suddenly stiffen slightly as Vax took control and then go into a complicated series of manoeuvres, the spare air tank puffing out little bursts of white vapour every now and again, and then finally the thump as he hit the side of the vessel knocking the breath out of him.

Luckily, or through good judgement on the part of his companion, he had arrived next to the hatchway, and a quick grip on a hand hold stopped him from bouncing off into space again.

With a great sigh of relief, Cresswell hurriedly opened the familiar hatch, crawled inside, pulled the hatch to and hit the air button.

There was a sharp hiss of air, a solid click, and then nothing.

'Oh god, the damn ship must have been hit by a meteorite and holed.' He realized the internal air had leaked out and the sensors have cut off the air supply to save wasting it.

'I can get in, but will still have to use my own air supply. I'll switch tanks now, as the old one must be nearly used up, also, it could take forever to find the leak.'

'Use a little logic. If the airlock is devoid of air after you try to fill it, then the leak must be in this area somewhere. If the ship is also devoid of air, then the chances are that the particle has gone through the hatch or an area near to it, and then gone on to make a hole in the wall between the hatch area and the internal ship. I suggest that you check this area first.'

'That's good thinking, I'm afraid I panicked there for a moment. I shall have to go into the main ship to get the patch kit, and then we'll hunt for the hole.'

The inner hatch opened without trouble, but there were no lights within the vessel.

'It looks as if the main power has been cut off as well. That could take a bit of restoring as I've never had to do that.'

'Let us effect a seal on the holes first so that you can work without your suit, I am sure we can restore power once we have an atmosphere to work in.'

With the repair kit quickly located, Cresswell returned to the airlock feeling a little more hopeful. Search as he might, he couldn't find the hole, and was getting quite desperate.

'May I suggest that you put your hand lamp on wide beam, leave it in the airlock and then go outside. The hole should show up as a tiny pin prick of light.

'To the rescue again! Of course you're right. It's a good idea, but I don't like the idea of going out again after all the trouble of getting in.'

The lamp was switched on, a reluctant Cresswell crawled out of the hatch, and the leak was found almost at once.

Going back into the airlock, Cresswell applied the patch to the hole in the door, looked at the opposite wall and found the other leak. With both holes sealed off, he then tried the air fill valve again, and this time it hissed its message of welcome, and within a short time the whole vessel was up to pressure.

The emergency lighting came on, although a little dimly, but it was enough for Cresswell to safely move about without bumping into things.

'I have never been so pleased to get my suit off.' Cresswell sighed, taking in a lung full fresh air, 'I have to thank you for your skill, and patience, when I lost mine.'

He almost felt his companion smile, or he thought that's what he felt.

'I don't understand how I've managed to last so long without food, and yet I haven't felt hungry until now.'

'I do not think we had time to feel anything apart from what was going on at the time, but you can now make up for the lost energy you need.'

Cresswell went to the food locker, and in the dim light withdrew a recon package. Inserting the water tube he waited for the requisite three minutes for the food to reform, and then opened the packet.

The first taste was enough to tell him that all was not well.

'It tastes awful, it must have gone off somehow, I'll try another one.' A different packet was chosen and reconstituted, but with the same result.

'I don't understand this. I've never had a bad food packet before and now we have two. Something has gone horribly wrong somewhere, I'll try one of the sealed units.'

The metal foil was stripped from a block of concentrate, and he bit cautiously into the dark brown mass.

'That tastes better, in fact it tastes normal, although a little salty, so what has happened to the rest of the supplies?'

'I do not know, perhaps we had better look at the time factor involved. Check the elapsed time indicator, that should tell us how long we have been away from the Tug.'

'You mean the clock, God it's stopped! Must have happened when the power went down, but it should keep going under its own power for years. Everything points to us having been off the tug for a very long time indeed. So, just how long have we been away?'

There was no answer.

The emergency power supply was very low, but was just able to light the screen for Cresswell to view the maintenance manual, something he had never bothered or needed to do before.

After a long and frustrating time, he managed to find the section relating to power management and the changing of fuel supplies to the unit, something which was always done back at the smelter station, and by someone else.

This led to the section on how to initiate the power generator after refuelling, and he thought applying that procedure should restore power to the tug. Which it did. The lights came back on, various pumps and other motors whirled into action, and the air tasted a little fresher after the filters had reduced the dust level to normal.

'Well, it looks as if we're back in business, but to do what? The asteroid is a no-go area, the normal food supply has gone off, so that will have to be replaced 'cos I'm not eating that solid concentrate for the next six months. Do we collect another mineral asteroid and return to the smelter, or just go back anyway to see what's happened to the ship?'

'I would suggest that a return journey without an addition to your credit account would be inefficient, so perhaps we could find something worthwhile to take back.'

The search for a suitable asteroid to take back to the orbiting smelter took a little longer than they thought, but one was finally located, and the mineral content checked out, and found not to be wanting.

Attaching the tow line to the asteroid went smoothly enough, and the long journey back to the smelter began, which left plenty of time for Cresswell and his companion to try and make some sense of the strange happenings which had befallen them since sighting the alien asteroid.

'Checking on some of the equipment on board, it would seem that a very long time indeed has passed since we left the tug to explore the alien ship, and that, if it were true, would account for the standard food packs deteriorating.

'To me, it seemed less than a day, but the tug power plant shut down, the clock stopped, the food packs went bad, and they are usually good for years, or so I'm told. The fabric of my sleep cover is weak and easily torn and what odd pieces of paper I left lying around have gone brown and brittle. All these things would point to a time period of about two hundred years or so, yet we were only away from the tug for a short time. What do you make of it Vax?'

'I have very little data to form my conclusions upon, but if I use the theory I have, then maybe we can make some sense of what has happened.

The alien ship was, I would think, travelling at light speed or even above light speed, and that would account for the strange effect it had on our viewing of the star field and the fact that the stars became invisible as velocity increased.

According to the theory, we would not have grown any older than we normally would, but because of the time dilation theory, time for others not travelling with us would have, from our point of view, grown older at an accelerated rate. By how much I can not calculate without the necessary data, which we do not have.

From the state of the tug, the distance the tug had moved away from the position we left it in, and the distance we must have travelled in the alien ship, I would guess that a figure of two to three hundred years would not be too unreal.'

'That means all the people I knew back at the smelter station are long dead, and no one will recognize me or even know about the tug.'

'That would seem likely, if my theory is correct. Why do you not use your radio communicator to call up the station, and tell them your clock has stopped and you need to know the time reference?'

'That's good thinking Vax,' and Cresswell switched on the communication unit, tuned in the station frequency and sent out his message.

All that could be heard on the incoming receiver was the wash of static, interspersed with the extra loud crackle and pop as something somewhere discharged a large amount of electrical energy, but they didn't know what it was.

He tried all the hailing frequencies, the emergency call line and even a random selection to try and get some response. There was nothing apart from the random noises he had heard before.

'There should be someone there, they can't have invented something better than the standard radio link, surely. I don't like the sound of this, it almost implies that there is no one at the station or even on earth, as I can usually get the main radio stations, even out here.'

Desperation began to flavour the otherwise calm tone of Cresswell's voice, and he felt the first pangs of panic begin to sweep over him like a dark black cloud as he realized he may now be alone in the universe as he knew it.

'I just can't believe this, surely it can't be true?'

'We shall only know for certain when we reach your earth orbit and can contact the smelter station directly, or even get some pictures up from the planet's surface.'

'Have you ever heard of this kind of thing happening before Vax? I mean, your people are far more advanced than mine.'

'Not as such. We travel just below the speed of light, and there is some distortion of time, but not on the scale that seems to have happened to us. This is a new experience for me as well, and I can understand your fear of what might have happened, but we do not have all the data relating to the event yet. Let us not panic at foregone conclusions which are based on partial data.'

Cresswell felt a little better from the calm attitude displayed by his companion, but the nagging fear of everything having changed beyond all possible reason still persisted at the back of his mind.

The tug continued on its way back to the smelter station with the mineral asteroid in tow, and apart from checking all the equipment on board to make sure it was functioning correctly, there was little else to do except re-examine the unbelievable possibilities of what seemed to have happened when on board the alien ship, and the consequences of what might follow.

Halfway back to the station he tried the radio link again, but was only rewarded by the constant stream of static and the occasional pop and crackle of an electric discharge, but they didn't last long enough for him to get a fix on them and so determine the direction from which they came.

As the tug swept into a parallel orbit with the smelter station, he began the tricky manoeuvre of swinging the asteroid around in a semicircle so that the breaking operation and the final approach to the docking bay could being.

Once more the radio link was tried, but the results were the same except that the pops and crackles were a little louder and Cresswell's sense of foreboding deepened.

With the asteroid now ahead of them and the tug under full deceleration, there was nothing to do until they picked up the homing beam which would guide them into the docking position, but the beam didn't come on.

Peering deeply into the scanner which was at full magnification, he could just make out the scintillating speck which he hoped was the station, but it was Vax who spotted the first piece of bad news.

'It looks as if the symmetry of the reflectors has changed, they were not like that when we left the station.'

'God, you're right. Something must have banged into them, only one looks as it should, the other two are bent or folded up. It must have happened recently or they would have been repaired. The station can't function without them.'

The lack of comment from his companion made Cresswell fear the worst. Perhaps they couldn't be repaired for some reason, and he really didn't want to speculate on the possible reasons for that.

As the tug drew nearer to the station it was plain to see that the reflector array was badly damaged, and there was no activity around the main docking bay which was usually alive with small craft doing maintenance or transferring materials for shipping down to earth.

Normally the station would have been lit up in a blaze of light, like a very expensive Christmas tree of old, but now there were just a few dull glows from maintenance lights behind the odd porthole.

The main guidance beam was still missing, as were all radio transmissions, and Cresswell had the dread feeling that that wasn't all that would be missing when they made their final contact.

Bringing the tug in manually was not the easiest of tasks, and after many heart stopping moments and a few words which Vax queried the meaning of, the job was completed, and Cresswell got ready to leave the tug and see what had happened to the station.

The first problem was that the automatic coupling of the tug to the entry hatch didn't happen. Again and again, Cresswell brought the tug up into position, and the auto lock system refused to respond.

'I'll have to leave the tug alongside and try the maintenance hatch, there's no other way in that I know of.'

'*Will the tug stay in position after we leave it? We may need to use it again.*'

'I'll uncouple the asteroid and use the tow line to anchor the tug to a stanchion, there are plenty of them around the work area.'

Letting go of the asteroid was the easy part of the job, getting the stiff cable around a stanchion and tied off firmly introduced Vax to a few new words, which he wisely thought he would query at a later and less fraught time.

Finally Cresswell was ready to enter the main station, and after locating the maintenance door and getting himself into the air lock, found that the inner door wouldn't open no matter how hard he pressed the opening button.

'*Is there a manual override to the doorway?*'

'I don't know. There should be.'

All Cresswell could find in the otherwise barren airlock was a small box-like structure beside the hatch, but there were no signs of a means of entry into it. Two new words were added to the list which Vax would query at a later date, but the hatch remained stubbornly closed.

'Do you have any instruments on board the tug with which to force the box open?'

'Yes I do, but I don't want the hassle of going to get them.'

In the end he had to give in to logic, went back to the tug and returned with an assortment of tools.

'Before you try to open the door, you had better seal the outer hatch.'

'Thanks Vax, what would I do without you! Sorry, I didn't mean to be sarcastic, it's just that I am afraid of what we may find, and I'm fast running out of patience.'

'I understand.'

The cover to the box-like structure finally gave way to his assault and exposed a handle and a series of old fashioned gear wheels.

'Looks like you're right. I don't see any other purpose for this collection of wheels other than to open the door.'

Turning the handle took all of Cresswell's strength and made him sweat. The old mechanism probably hadn't been used since the station had been built, even if then.

At long last there were a series of faint clicks as the locking lugs released and a sigh from the seals as the pressure came off them.

Gathering up the tools in case he needed them again, he pulled open the hatch and stepped into the deserted smelter station.

With the hatch closed behind him, and fear eating away at the pit of his stomach, Cresswell headed off in the direction of the main stores in the dim glow of the emergency lights.

One of the few things which man had managed to create with a degree of eternity to them, were the emergency lights.

Formed from long rods of doped quartz, they gave a low level of light from an electric current that was almost impossible to measure, so efficient were they.

As there were no filaments or gases to burn out, they were considered to be just about indestructible, and carried on working as long as there was a small flow of electrons to excite the doped atoms.

Cresswell's first concern was to locate a supply of breathing packs, as the section of the station he had entered was de-pressurized, and as far as he knew, so was the rest of it.

He would also have to restock the tug for future use.

The stores door opened easily enough, and he crawled through the hatchway to the inner section. It wasn't long before he found what he was looking for.

'It's going to take some time to get a few of these to the outer hatchway, but I think we may need them later, and if we have to leave in a hurry, I don't want to have to mess about here lugging these things around.'

'That seems very sensible. You must also replace your food stocks as well. May I would suggest that you collect the most concentrated type available, as they will take up the least amount of space.'

Cresswell made a face at the thought of the concentrates, which brought a mental chuckle from his companion.

Some thirty minutes later, Cresswell had a good supply of foods, enough breathing packs to last half a life time and an assortment of tools to add to his collection on the tug, although he didn't know where he was going, or why, at the present.

'I must go up to the observatory, from there we should get a good view of earth and perhaps we can find out what's been going on.'

With the auto walkways out of action, and no elevators operational, it was a long haul up to the observatory, but he eventually got there, albeit a little out of breath.

Fortunately, all the electrically driven controls had a manual override, and so he was able to bring the telescope into line with earth, and then focus it.

'Can't see much. Just clouds and more clouds. There's the occasional flash of light which could mean there's a city below, and a break in the clouds allows the lights to show through. Difficult to tell really.'

'Can we view the other two stations? Maybe we could get some idea of their state, and from that deduce what might have happened.'

'No, you can't see them from here, they're around the other side of earth. The sun should come around fully soon, and then we'll be able to see more detail.'

A while later the sun began to shine on the huge world before them, but the only extra detail they could see was a little more of the clouds, most areas of which were darker and more menacing than he had expected.

'It looks as if the weather has changed considerably from how I remember it. The whole earth seems to be covered in greyish cloud, when usually it is mostly pale blue and white.'

There being nothing else he could do in the observatory, Cresswell returned to the lower levels in search of clues which might lead to a reason for the desertion of the station.

There were no signs of panic or fighting, or even the odd body lying about, just no personnel in the station.

Everything seemed to have been abandoned, and most equipment had been shut down before being left.

'The exit seems to have been orderly, so attack from another station or outside force doesn't seem to have been the cause, so why would they give up one of their most precious possessions?'

'We may have to go down to earth to find the answer to that. Can we do that?'

'Yes, I suppose so, but not in the tug, that only operates in space, so we'll have to find a shuttle craft and then the next problem is that I don't know how to fly one of those.'

Some sections of the smelter station were inaccessible to Cresswell, either the doors were locked or they had been damaged in some way, so although he was able to replenish his supplies, he was unable to access some of the data he wanted, that was held on the main computers in the administration section.

'Pity I can't get in there, I could give my credit account a good boost while I was at it.'

'It would be of little avail to do so if things are as bad on earth as they are here.'

'I was only making a joke.' Cresswell retorted, realizing that his companion lacked what he thought of as a subtle sense of humour.

'There's little more we can do here, so I suppose we had better try to find a shuttle and get down to earth to see what's happened to it.'

The lower levels of the station contained the docking bays for tugs and their mineral loads, but he couldn't find the area from which the earth to station shuttles were docked and housed.

'It's been so long since I came up here that I can't remember where I entered the station, but there must be an embarkation point here somewhere.'

'Can you remember what you did when you came up here for the first time?'

'I only came up here once, and I've never left except to go and get asteroids.'

'What did you do upon arriving here?'

'I went to a reception area where I signed the contract for tug duty. Right. I'm ahead of you.'

'I doubt that,' echoed very faintly in Cresswell's mind.

The main reception hall didn't look as if it was the place where he first came into the station, so he began the long job of searching every corridor on that level to find the one small office which he was now able to recall as his starting point of a long career in space mining.

At long last he found something which seemed familiar, a small room with a big tri-dimensional picture of the asteroid belt upon one wall, he remembered that as he was very impressed by its reality at the time.

'I think this is it, I remember seeing that picture on the wall. I came in through that door at the back there.'

Going around the desk he opened the door, and went through to a long sloping tunnel which eventually led out into a small docking bay.

Three embarkation hatches were spaced along one wall, and all were firmly closed. As the station was on emergency lighting only, there were no status lights to show what condition the shuttle hatches were in, or even if there was a shuttle present at any position on the other side.

'Even if we find a shuttle, I have no experience of flying one, and as for the actual landing, that could be suicide.'

'I feel sure that between us we can effect a safe landing on earth, the main difficulty is finding a usable shuttle.'

'The only thing I can do is try to open the hatches and see if there is anything on the other side of them, although I very much doubt if there is, they would have all been used for the exodus.'

The first hatch refused to open no matter how hard Cresswell tried, and that included a few hefty blows with a large wrench. The second one did open, and he nearly fell out into space due to the momentum he picked up from the opening door and the very low gravity.

A very quick reaction on the part of Vax caused his fingers to clasp the edge of the hatchway with a grip of steel, later provoking a complaint from Cresswell due to strained muscles.

Attaching his safety line to the hatch, he pushed himself out into space so as to get a good view of the area in which the hatches were situated, but there were no shuttles present that he could see.

'Looks like we're here to stay without transport, unless you can come up with something I haven't thought of.'

'Let me use your eyes again,' and before Cresswell could say anything he felt them screw up into elongated plums, and the terrible pain began once more.

I think I can see something out there which may be a shuttle, it looks like the long dart shape you remembered from the past.'

'God, I wish that didn't hurt so much, how the hell do you do it?'

All thoughts of a shuttle had disappeared as he longed to rub his aching eyes, but was prevented from doing so because of the helmet.

'I just take control of the muscles and make them work to my commands, I am sorry about the pain you feel, but there is no other way if I am to see into the far distance.'

'Sorry to moan, but you have no idea what that feels like. I suppose it means another jump off into space like we did before?'

'Yes, unless you can think of another way to get there.'

'I'll get a new propulsion unit and a couple of spares just in case we need them. If the shuttle is useless, we'll have to get back here.'

It would have been a long walk and a lot of hard work to retrieve the stores and three propulsion units and get them to the exit hatch in the passenger bay, so Cresswell decided to use the hatch where he had entered the station in the first place, and then jet around the hulk until he reached the passenger entry point.

From there he would have to rely on Vax being able to pick out the distant shuttle, and hopefully guide him to it.

The stores and the two extra propulsion units were lashed together in a rather untidy bundle, and he launched himself out of the open hatch, feeling once more, as he always did for a moment, that gut wrenching sensation as he drifted into nothingness.

Vax gave directions from memory for a while, and then warned Cresswell he was going to use his eyes again. Before he could complain, Vax had done the necessary, and given new directions.

Once the silver dart shape of the shuttle came into view, he could feel himself relax a little, but having misjudged his velocity, he bumped into the hull, and made a frantic grab for the open hatch.

'Doesn't look good the hatch being open, it must have been abandoned due to some fault I would think.'

There was no answer from Vax as Cresswell pulled himself into the airlock, closed the outer door and pressed the air valve.

He couldn't believe his luck as the valve hissed its message of greeting, and at long last he could hear his footsteps as he moved around.

Once air pressure was up to normal, he opened the inner door and entered the shuttle proper.

Walking up through the long line of passenger seats, memories of the time he came up to the station came flooding back, the excitement of the flight up, the magnificent sight of the massive station with it's giant light catching arrays, the smooth efficiency of the crew and eventually the beginning of a new life out in space.

Reaching the door to the control cabin, he hesitated for a moment, and then went in. All seemed to be in order as far as he could tell, but then he didn't know what to look for with regard to faults in the craft.

Seating himself at the controls he ran his fingers over the various instruments, trying to associate them with those on the tug. Having recognized several as being similar to those he was used to, he felt better about the whole idea of flying the machine back to earth.

Only one thing really worried him, why had the shuttle been abandoned when all of them would have been needed to ferry the crews back to earth? Also, was there enough fuel on-board, and how could he tell if there was?

'Do not worry so much. We have made good progress so far, let us see what else we can do.

You could try switching on the power unit which drives this vessel, there maybe some indication of the fuel level then.'

Cresswell checked over the controls, isolated what he thought should be the correct ones for the test, and decided it was worth a try. What had they to lose?

A low resonance sounded throughout the ship, more of the indicators lit up and Cresswell felt a little more confident about the whole thing.

Scanning the instruments located the fuel gauge, and beyond his wildest dreams it registered full.

'It must have been refuelled just before they left, as most of the fuel is used in getting up here, only a small amount is needed for the return trip.'

'We are fortunate indeed.'

'It would seem so, but why would they fill her to the limit when it isn't necessary for the return trip. It would cost so much more to refuel here, as it has to be brought up in the first place. There's something else we don't know about, where else could they have gone?'

'The other stations perhaps?'

'I doubt that. There was always such deep rivalry between them. They'd have cut each others throats given half a chance. This ship is only meant to ferry people to and fro from earth, it's no good for deep space travel, so it can't be that.'

'Let us see if we can manoeuvre the ship, and then we shall know if it is possible to go down. I may, if you don't mind, have to take control

if events become beyond your capabilities. That is not questioning your skills, merely putting our resources together. We both need to survive.'

Cresswell tried to swallow his hurt pride, found it stuck in his throat, swallowed hard and reached for the controls.

The vibration under his feet intensified a little and the shuttle moved slowly away from the station.

Cresswell's confidence grew in leaps and bounds as he swung the sleek ship around in a long curve, bringing the station back into view, and then sent it down in a long sweep towards the cloud covered planet below.

The controls were not too dissimilar to those of the tug, the only difference he could see were the control surfaces for atmospheric flight, and that he had never experienced.

As they dropped lower, the clouds took on a dark and more ominous tone, covering the surface of the planet in a dingy grey blanket, only the occasional glimpse of sea or land coming into view every now and again.

'Looking at the design of this ship, and the controls at your disposal, I would think the principle of entering the atmosphere would be to put the craft at an oblique angle and let the increasing air density act as a breaking force.'

'That makes good sense. I expect it's done automatically with the right pilot, but I'm not sure how to switch on the automatics. I'll increase the angle of attack and see what happens.'

The craft tilted slightly upwards from its flight path, and the buffeting of the denser air caused Cresswell's teeth to rattle.

Very gradually they lost altitude and the forward velocity decreased, but the bone jarring buffeting didn't.

'The craft is heating up by the look of that readout.'

'I think the craft is designed to accept that, do not let the readout go into that red area, I think that could mean danger for us.'

'I'll try not to, but how the hell do I stop it?' Cresswell's voice had a distinct quaver to it as he wrestled with the controls.

'Increase your angle of attack to the air.'

The shuttle approached the top of several giant black thunder heads which pierced the upper layers of the atmosphere, the lightning flashes lighting up the control cabin in a series of lurid purple and white flashes.

Occasionally vast streamers of energy leapt upwards from the top of the tormented cloud layer to reach out into space, fading as their energy dissipated.

Soon they were within the actual cloud band, lightning flashing all around them, but soundless, as the moans and groans of the craft itself overwhelmed all else. Tortured metal creaked and tinged as it tried to take up the strain of the over heating outer skin of the shuttle, which desperately tried to pass the added energy on to cooler parts.

'Somehow we must get below this cloud layer or we'll not be able to choose our landing area, and I don't fancy a dunking in the sea.'

'If you use the main engines carefully, you should be able to keep it flying until we see a suitable landing area.'

They flew on, blind to everything except the swirling grey clouds, and then a brief flash of a white topped mountain.

'We have land,' exclaimed Cresswell, a sigh of relief in his voice, 'but god knows where it is, and we need a long flat area put this thing down on.'

The altimeter indicated that they were now only a few thousand metres above the surface of the planet, and a landing site would have to be found soon.

A range of dirty snow capped mountains raced towards them, and then were gone, to be replaced by a vast expanse of dull grey ocean, heaving like a living creature in extreme pain. A rain squall obscured their view for a few moments and then they were through it and out into clear blue skies.

'I think a small pulse on the main engines would be a good idea as we are losing altitude quite quickly now.'

Cresswell was thrown back into his seat as the main thrusters came on, the shuttle nosing up a little and gaining speed.

On the far horizon a thin smear of coastline divided the now darkening sky and the turgid ocean, and as the shuttle raced towards it, details of the remains of a large town came into view.

It had once been a great city, but now not one building stood intact, rubble lay piled about in great untidy heaps spilling over to cover what was once a great arterial road system, only traces of which could now be made out beneath the detritus of destruction.

'How one group of people can do this to another beats any understanding I can muster. What is the point of it?'

'That is the point, there is none. I would think from listening to your communications over a long period, that communication itself, or the lack of it, has brought all this about. I can understand your sadness. I am very sorry.'

The shuttle skimmed over the remains of a shattered forest of huge proportions, all the trees were lying down in countless rows, pointing in the same direction like little sticks some mindless child had laid out because it couldn't think of an interesting pattern.

A range of low hills forced him to brace himself as another burst of the thrusters lifted the shuttle up a little to clear the barrier, and then before them lay a great plain of bare earth and sand.

'We're going down.' Cresswell yelled unnecessarily, habit forcing him to raise his voice because of the raucous noise of the shuttle cleaving the air.

The shuttle dipped lower and the bare ground raced up at a frightening speed.

A shudder went through the craft, and he realized that Vax had taken over momentarily to activate the landing gear as they skimmed over the barren wastes below.

A series of back breaking bumps signalled the fact that they had made contact with the surface, and the shuttle slowly lost speed and groaned to a halt.

'Well, that was a lot easier than I expected, and it looks as if we're down in one piece.'

'We can not be sure until we have examined the outside of the vehicle, the landing gear may have been damaged and that would preclude our leaving here.'

'I don't intend leaving now that we're down. This is my home world, and if I can find a nice quiet little corner here, I'm going to spend the rest of my days in it, and to hell with asteroid collecting.'

'I wonder if you will have the option to do as you choose. We had better assess the conditions here before we make any hard and fast decisions.'

'What's this 'we' business? it's my body and I decide where we go.'

There was no reply, so Cresswell dropped the subject, realizing that he had made an unnecessary and hurtful statement which wasn't valid, and wasn't really meant.

'Right, let's go see what we have out there.'

'Do you wish to test the air out there first?'

'Better had. Just thought of something. There's no disembarking trolley, so how do I get down, and more importantly, how do I get back up again if I need to?'

'You have a quantity of strong cord around your supplies, you could use that.'

'Well done Vax, good thing I've got you.' Cresswell hoped he didn't sound too condescending, but he did want to make up for his earlier unfortunate remark.

The outer hatch opened a few millimetres with a slight hiss as the internal atmosphere balanced its pressure with that of the outside world, and he eased it open a little more.

'I'll just ease the airlock on the helmet, and take a sniff to see if it's all right.' The first sniff caused Cresswell to wrinkle his nose, but he soon got used to the dank mouldy smell of mother earth's rotting vegetation and tortured atmosphere, and removed his helmet.

Removing his space suit added a spring to his step, and he was in an almost cheerful mood as he repackaged his supplies ready for a journey of discovery.

The shuttle had come to rest on the far edge of the plain, and it was to that edge he decided to go.

The ground was rough and torn, looking as if it had been roughed up by some giant maniacal plough with no idea of straight lines or symmetry. The going was tough, and Cresswell was soon tired as his muscles were not used to such rough treatment.

Sitting down to take the weight of his backpack off his shoulders, he idly poked around in the ground with his foot until it hit something hard.

A bit of scraping and a good hard tug revealed the remains of a cylindrical shape which had been torn and twisted by what could only have been an explosive force from within.

'This looks like some kind of missile, but it is crudely fashioned, just look at the rivets along this edge, as though those who made it couldn't form a continuous tube.'

'It certainly does not look as if it had been made by an advanced race like yours, maybe their manufacturing abilities have been curtailed by the conflict and this is the best they can do.'

'That seems hard to believe, but you may well be right.'

Cresswell plodded on towards what looked like the remains of a wooded area, although only the bare stumps could be seen from where he was and the ground was littered with the protruding riven remains of what were once thick majestic branches.

Reaching the edge of the shattered forest, Cresswell looked around for some sign of human habitation, but there was nothing in sight which vaguely looked like a dwelling, much less any human beings.

There were, in the distance, a small group of trees which still bravely held a few tattered branches aloft in defiance of whatever force had devastated the area, and Cresswell headed for them to find a small cluster of rocks formed the abutment from which the mutilated trees had sprung, and formed a natural hiding place for anyone wishing to observe without being seen.

'I think I'll lie low for a few moments to get my breath back, and see if there is anything living in this area.'

'I think a rest would be a good idea, your muscles are not used to such exertion, and need to be built up slowly to avoid strain.'

Cresswell nestled down between two rocks so that only the top of his head peered over a thick twisted branch, giving him a good view of the plain area and the remains of the pulverized wood on either side.

After several minutes rest, he managed to get his eyes back into focus and the sweat had stopped streaming down his forehead. There had been no movement out on the plain, no bird, animal or creature of any kind, and Cresswell was beginning to get a nasty feeling in his stomach.

'There's no sign of life anywhere, and that's worrying. There should be something moving about, an insect or bird, but there's nothing at all.'

'There is something moving over there on your right.'

'I can't see anything, what is it?'

'Let me use...... The pain this time wasn't so bad, and he tried to relax as Vax twisted his eyeballs into the necessary elongated shape.

'It seems to be mechanical by its movement compared to what I have seen of your creatures, but then that is not very much. Wait until it gets a little nearer, I think it is coming this way.'

Cresswell strained his eyes after he got them back, and suddenly he was able to make out an odd looking shape crawling along the ground ahead and to one side of him.

'I think you're right. It looks like a box with ears and a tail, moving on linked tracks. There's a small plume of pale blue smoke coming out of the back of it. Good god, what have they resorted to now?'

'I do not know, but it is a strange device even for your people.' Cresswell wondered if Vax was 'getting one back' for a moment, but then dismissed the idea, Vax was far too practical for such things.

Four:
Of Wheels and Oil

ON THE BROW of a distant ridge, a boxy object could be seen trundling its way down towards the beginning of the long slope where Cresswell stood.

There was no sound, just little puffs of dust as it scurried along, and a faint trace of bluish smoke trailing behind it.

He stood fascinated as the object crept its way downwards, lurching from side to side as it hit some rougher parts of the terrain

As it drew nearer, a soft 'thub-thub' could be heard from what was possibly an engine, or a very lose piece of metal banging in time to the swaying motion of the strange looking device.

Slowly the metal contraption clanked and rattled its way across the plain before them, going at a good walking pace and obviously intent on some indefinable purpose.

There was a faint whistling noise which grew louder, and then a thump and a plume of smoke and debris leapt into the air just in front of the moving box thing.

He jumped, the box spun around on its tracks and headed straight for him.

Another whistle and a thump, and the box was no longer a box, but a collection of metallic bits and pieces rising up into the air in a thick black cloud of smoke, and raining back to earth as the smoke drifted away to one side.

'I almost feel sorry for it.' was all Cresswell could say, swallowing hard.

'Who or whatever sent that missile, was a very good shot, so how come they haven't had a go at us? We were in full view of whatever it was as we crossed the plain, and I'm sure if it can hit that box, it must be capable of seeing and hitting us.'

'*One thing does not necessarily lead to another, that was one mechanical thing attacking another mechanical thing, you are flesh and blood, and so may not count as a target.*

I would think the missile probably uses a heat seeking device to detect its target, and your body does not generate enough heat for it to pick up.'

'You mean the silly sods have resorted to making little robots to fight the other side's little robots? What possible purpose could that achieve?'

'I do not know, I am thankfully not a human being, so can not equate events and their needs as do your people, but it is a sad state of affairs if it has come to this.'

'Do you think it would be safe to go out there to see what remains of the box, and so get some idea of what it's all about?'

'I think it is safe enough, as you say, we have not been targeted, and there have been plenty of chances for an assailant to strike if it wished to do so.'

Cresswell eased himself out of his hiding place and cautiously moved towards the remains of the mechanical box device that was.

A smell of hot oil and the acrid smoke of a crude explosive still hung in the still air and intensified as he drew close to the shattered remains of the mechanical contraption.

The twisted remains lay scattered over a considerable distance, showing that the explosive was at least efficient in its work, even if a bit smelly.

'It looks like a rather crude compression ignition engine, burning an even cruder thick oil as fuel, and I'm surprised it worked as well as it did. The whole thing seems to have been cobbled together from odd bits and pieces, rivets being the main means of securing the separate parts together.'

Cresswell ferreted among the still smoking wreckage, looking for something which would give him a clue as to why such things were roaming the remains of the countryside, and to what purpose.

'What do you think that device was?' He felt his eyes being turned to look at a dented cylinder with a series of pipes attached to it.

'Difficult to say for certain, but this bit looks like a pump, and these are delivery tubes. Perhaps the container holds a burnable fuel, and the intention is to spray hot fuel over whatever it needs to burn. A rather crude way to attack an enemy. But where is the target? I haven't seen anything worth attacking since we've been down here.'

'The target may only be a target in the eyes of the attacker, and that depends upon what the attacker decides is worth attacking. I sense something else on the move, better for us to get back into the trees.'

Little encouragement was needed for Cresswell to high tail it back to the trees, and tuck himself almost out of sight behind the remains of a stump. He didn't have long to wait.

There was a just discernible trembling in the ground beneath his feet, and he looked around for the cause. There was nothing in sight, and that unnerved him a little.

A hundred metres or so out on the plain the ground seemed to be moving of its own accord, not a great deal, but just enough to be observed out of the corner of his eye.

The rippling motion stopped and a small tube like protuberance with a knob on the top rose up for about two metres, turned a complete circle, and then withdrew to below ground level.

Once again, the gentle tremble of the ground began and gradually grew fainter and fainter, while a faint haze of water vapour arose from the disturbed ground behind the burrower.

Several whistles and their accompanying explosions followed, which only served to rearrange the already tortured earth, but they were well off their intended target, which continued to cause a slight ripple on the surface of the earth as it burrowed its way along.

'There's one that got away.' exclaimed Cresswell, sounding almost pleased, but that was short lived.

A thin dirty blue grey line began to curve up from the horizon, and as it drew nearer he could just make out a whirling shape at its head. The thuck thuck of rotating blades grew louder as the device approached the clump of trees and then veered off to follow the line in the ground made by the burrower.

A slight gust of wind blew the exhaust smoke away from the contraption for a moment, and Cresswell could clearly see what it was.

A box shape, about the size of a man was hung beneath a series of rotating blades, not all of which were symmetrical by the uneven noise it was making. The thing hovered over the spot where the burrower had halted and was having a very hard time of it trying to hold the position against the breeze.

He squatted there open mouthed in amazement behind his tree trunk as the scene unfolded.

The burrower had extended its long tube with the knob on the end, and it was searching for the source of the noise over head. Then a second more business-like tube extended itself from the burrower, and swung around to point directly at the hovering flying machine overhead.

A little jet of flame and a puff of blackish smoke from the second tube signalled that a missile had been fired upwards, and simultaneously the hovering machine dropped a dark object from its belly.

The two objects passed each other only centimetres apart and reached their respective targets in the same instant.

The hovering machine flew apart in a ringing jangling display of flying blades, the box like structure which had supported them tumbling over and over as it raced towards the ground.

The burrower had received a direct hit on the 'looking tube' mounting, and was now churning up the ground as it crawled out of its hole and blindly propelled itself around in a circle, it's steering mechanism crippled.

'This is bloody impossible! I just can't believe it! A bunch of machines mindlessly fighting another bunch of machines. It's a god-damned nightmare.'

Any further thoughts on the matter were interrupted by a clanking puffing noise which grew in intensity over the next few minutes.

Over the brow of the low hill to Cresswell's left, a large box on clanking caterpillar tracks heaved itself along, heading straight for the stricken burrower.

A tall chimney belched black smoke intermingled with white steam as the monstrosity lumbered along, churning up the ground more efficiently than a conventional plough could ever have done.

Approaching the stricken burrower, the new machine extended a flail like rod from its front end and began to beat the burrower as it cavorted around in ever diminishing circles.

Finally the burrower gave up under the onslaught, or had its traction unit beaten into submission, for it just squatted there, twitching in its death throws.

The flail withdrew and folded itself neatly away, and then a long grab arm extended itself, sharp metal teeth glinting on its end, and swiftly scooped up the burrower, swivelled around, and dropped it into the box like structure at the rear end of the vehicle.

With several large puffs of steam, a squeal of metal on dry metal, machine turned around, groping about in the churned up earth for the body of the flying machine which had fallen nearby.

Having found it, the machine unceremoniously dropped it into the collecting box on its rear end and trundled off in the direction it had come in.

'This really is too much, it's impossible!' Cresswell ran out of words to express his feelings.

'I can understand your inability to comprehend the situation as it is so foreign to your way of thinking, but may I suggest what I think might have happened, based on what little information I have been able to gather?'

'Yes, please go ahead, it can't be any more bizarre than what I've just seen.'

'It would seem that a great war must have broken out among your people, and as the number of humans dwindled, the remaining ones constructed factories to produce machines to do the fighting for them. These factories must have had a degree of self preservation and replication built into them, for they have continued to do battle long after any needed to do so. They are unthinking in the sense we use, they just do what they have been programmed to do, and will continue to do so until they annihilate each other completely or run out of materials, hence the last machine we saw, collecting up the remains of the damaged devices.'

'Why didn't our shuttle get attacked when we landed?'

'I would think it may be due to its construction or maybe the type of exhaust gasses emitted. We landed without using the engines, and although the mass of the shuttle may have been picked up, perhaps it did not meet a certain criteria which was necessary to delineate it as being a member of an opposing force. This is only conjecture, as I do not have enough data to be certain. I would think that we could travel about here with impunity as we do not constitute a threat to these machines. As far as they are concerned, we do not exist, which is fortunate for us.'

Cresswell sat back in his hidey hole among the rocks, trying to digest the seemingly impossible, and getting mental indigestion for his troubles.

'Do you really think there are no humans left?'

'I would doubt it, or this insanity would be stopped as it serves little purpose, but then again, your people often do things for little purpose which I can understand.'

'So what do we do now? Is there any point in staying here, and if not, where do we go?'

'As we are here, it might be interesting to see just how advanced these machines are, and if they will ever cease their warring. Just maybe we can do something to stop the conflict, although I doubt we can. I would suggest that we follow the trail left by the collecting vehicle, and see where it leads. If there is an automated factory, I would certainly like to see it.'

'Well, there's little else to do, so I suppose we may as well.' Cresswell felt saddened and dejected to a degree he didn't know could happen, what hope for humanity now?

They left the little clump of rocks with their covering of sad and battered trees, and set off in the furrow left by the collecting vehicle.

It was easy to follow as the rough ground had been compacted flat by the sheer weight of the machine, and it had left a very distinct track across the edge of the plain for as far as they could see. Several times a flying machine clattered by overhead, and Cresswell instinctively ducked and looked for somewhere to hide much to the amusement of Vax, who teased him about it each time one went by.

'They are not interested in us, relax and concentrate on your footing.'

'It's all right for you, I've got years of habit to overcome, and that's not easy.'

Once they had to stop and leave the trail as a small fast moving vehicle came up from behind following in the same track they were using.

It rattled by, a box-like structure mounted on three sets of caterpillar track, squeaking and clanking, and bristling with an array of tubes and rods sticking out in all directions.

'That one looks as if it is equipped to handle anything from any direction at any time by the amount of armament on it,' commented Cresswell as it brushed by him.

'It certainly looks well equipped, and I would think it is on the trail of the collecting vehicle, no doubt programmed to retrieve the burrower and anything else it can get.'

'I doubt if I can keep pace with it, but I'll try.' panted Cresswell as he broke into a run.

Immediately he felt a restraining sensation in his leg muscles.

'I would suggest you keep a safe distance behind it as it is likely to be attacked by the opposing side once it is detected.'

Shortly afterwards, two flying machines appeared and were promptly shot down in a hail of tiny missiles from the three tracked vehicle, which hardly paused in its rattling journey up the track.

Several bits of metal fell to earth near Cresswell, and he dropped back a few paces to be on the safe side in case of further attacks.

The three tracker had gained some distance on a panting Cresswell as he mounted the crest of the slope and looked down on the shattered land below.

The remains of an old road threaded its way across the area ahead from left to right, and the three trackers had found this and followed it faithfully for several hundred metres before coming to an unexpected halt. The track left by the collecting vehicle had also joined the old road, and Cresswell stopped to see what would happen next, as there was an uncanny feeling of expectancy in the air.

A deep throbbing noise which grew louder every second, drew

Cresswell's attention to the sky above the three tracker.

This time, someone or something really meant business. The flying machine was much bigger than the previous two had been, and with two sets of rotors whirling and clattering above a chunky body which Cresswell estimated to be about ten metres long.

'We must be getting near something very important for heavy armaments like this to be brought into play.'

'Yes, and I don't think that little three tracker is going to stand much of a chance against that airborne unit, it's massive.'

'Size is not always a criteria to go by, let us see what happens.'

The twin rotored machine carefully positioned itself above the three tracker and then lowered a cable attached to the end of which was a large oblong casing with three tubes sticking out beneath it.

As the object on the end of the cable drew nearer to the three tracker, it suddenly sprouted two huge heavy gauge sheets of metal which swung up to form a sloping roof above the vehicle.

The oblong object was within half a metre of the now protecting roof of the three tracker, when it belched three streams of flame downwards, engulfing the little vehicle from end to end in a sizzling blaze of heat.

The flames died down after several minutes, and the little three tracker was still there, smoking a little, but intact.

The flying machine then dropped several bomb-like objects, some of which hit the protecting roof and glanced off to explode harmlessly to one side. Those which landed close to the three tracker sent huge plumes of dirt into the air, but the three tracker stood firm under the onslaught.

'It must have sent roots down not to have been toppled over by that barrage.'

'That is what I was thinking. Somehow these machines learn from past experience and take the necessary action not to fail in the same situation again, should it occur.'

The flying machine seemed to pause for thought, and that was its fatal mistake.

The hinged roof section of the three tracker opened just enough for six tube like extensions to peek out, and then a barrage of fire poured forth that made him jump back, although he was well out of range of any falling debris.

The staccato scream of hundreds of small missiles hurt Cresswell's ears as the flying machine shuddered under the intense hail of fire from the three tracker, who having spent its ammunition, promptly closed its roof section over again as if waiting for the inevitable retaliation.

Pieces of the flying machine rained down for several moments while it gyrated about trying to stabilize itself and adjust to the imbalance due to so much of it having been torn away by the barrage.

Eventually the engine gave a series of deep coughs and the whole thing came crashing down in a tangled heap to one side of the three tracker, who by now had withdrawn its stabilizing rods and continued on up the track as though nothing had happened.

'I know I've said it before, but it's bloody unbelievable, all this mechanical warring, the damn things seem to be almost intelligent.'

'I know what you mean, but it is only very clever programming, and a built in system of learning from past mistakes, it is not intelligence in the true sense of the word.'

Cresswell hastened after the three tracker as it lumbered on, its speed now reduced for some reason, so he was able to keep up with it without getting too exhausted.

They cleared the next ridge and were then confronted by a change of scenery. Ahead was a massive cliff reaching up several hundred metres and the track led right up to the base of it. Between them and the cliff was a deep moat or trench with earth piled high on the far side, the bottom of the trench being filled with water of unknown depth.

'It looks as if we have arrived at a place of some importance by the size of the defence trench, something does not want others to encroach upon its territory.'

'How do we get across that?' asked Cresswell, seeing no obvious route.

'Let us see what the three tracker does, maybe it or its predecessor has had some experience of this problem.'

The three tracker went right up to the edge of the chasm, paused for a while, and then backed up a little.

By now, he had moved up much closer and was able to watch in some detail how the machine worked.

A metallic arm extended itself from the back of the vehicle, and drove itself deep down into the earth until only a short section was visible. A cable attached to the tracker was also attached to the rod, and the tracker then eased itself over the edge of the trench and lowered itself down on a winch until it almost reached the water.

Cresswell had moved up to the edge of the trench and peered over to gasp in amazement at the tracker's next move.

Two inflatable bags grew out of the side of the tracker, and it then dropped the last few centimetres to the surface of the water, and floated.

A forward facing tube suddenly angled upwards, disgorged a cloud of smoke and half a dozen missiles attached to thin cords. These streaked upwards to fly over the top of the trench and land behind the earthworks.   A series of muffled explosions followed as the devices drove themselves deeply into the earth, and the tracker now had a means of hauling itself out of the trench.

Slowly, but very surely, the tracker heaved itself up the side of the trench by winding in the cords, and soon it was atop the earth works and heading on towards the cliff.

'The cords are still in place, is it worth risking?'

'Yes, I think you could climb out of the trench, but be careful crossing the water, we do not know if it is corrosive.'

'God, I didn't think of that, I'll check it.'

Cresswell slid down the first cable stopping just before he hit the water, and dipped a finger into it. As it didn't burn or give any other strange sensations, he gingerly touched it to his lips and then pronounced it safe.

Pulling himself across by the cable was the easy part, but he needed Vax to add a little extra command to his muscles to climb up the trench side and reach the earthworks.

By now the tracker had reached nearly half way to the cliff, and with a little squeeze from Vax, he could see that there was some activity going on at the base of the cliff, and a dark entrance hole he hadn't noticed before.

Dotted about the area in front of him, were a random collection of stone blocks, piled upon one another to form a series of pyramids, some larger than others.

'Do you think they are to stop vehicles?' asked Cresswell, as he could see no other reason for them being there.

'I do not think so, as they are too far apart to be effective as a barrier, I do not know what they are for, but we will soon see if they are part of the defence system.'

'That tracker certainly doesn't give up easily, does it?'

'It is programmed to do what it has to, and will carry on doing so until stopped. I shall be interested to see how the opposing force reacts to such

a close approach.'

Cresswell hurried on down the earth slope and onto the compacted track left by the collection vehicle, making speedy travel so much easier.

'I think we should move over to one side now, as the defending devices at the cliff face may over shoot the target and hit us.'

He needed no second bidding, and leapt for the safety of the rougher ground to the left of the track, and only just in time.

The three tracker had now adopted a strange strategy, frequently changing the speed back and forth as it advanced down the track so that anything aiming at it could not know precisely where it would be when a missile landed.

'Now that I call clever.' commented Cresswell, admiration showing in his voice.

'Do not be misled, it is only programming based on past experience. They, whoever they are, must have lost an awful lot of vehicles before they got this far, learning from each one no doubt.'

The three tracker had now changed its method of advancement yet again, swinging from side to side of the track as it also changed speed. Any tracking device would have had a very hard time of it trying to predict where it would be at any given time, and so aiming a missile at it would not guarantee a hit.

Several explosive charges went off around the tracker, but none hit the target as it danced its way towards the cliff.

'The defenders are a bit half-hearted about their attack.' commented Cresswell.

'Perhaps they are a little low on ammunition.'

Without warning, a section of the cliff slid to one side and a row of squat little truck like vehicles raced forward, black smoke pouring from their exhaust stacks as they laboured under the heavy load of what looked like a massive block of stone or concrete mounted on the front of each of them.

The little trucks formed a loose semicircle in front of the advancing tracker, closing ranks as the distance decreased.

For a moment the tracker seemed confused, and then it raced forward in a straight line, no doubt hoping to break through the line before it could close, and offer a solid stone wall defence.

It was too late, the stone bearing trucks had little space between them now, and the three tracker smashed into one of them and came to a shuddering halt.

The other trucks quickly circled around the tracker, and deposited their stones to surround it, building a solid barricade to prevent any movement in any direction, and then proceeded to pile more stones on top.

Before long, all that could be seen was a neat pile of stone blocks, just like all the others dotted about the plain, the tracker being held in place by sheer weight.

One by one the little trucks formed up into a line and returned to the cliff, going into the hole from which they had come out, and the entrance remained open, much to their surprise.

'What a pity, I feel almost sorry for the tracker, it nearly made it.'

'True, but it now gives us a chance to see what is going on inside the cliff, for I would assume that is where all the manufacturing is done.'

'We go in? asked an anxious Cresswell.

'Yes, I do not see any danger as long as we keep clear of moving machinery, they will not recognize us as a threat.'

'God, I hope you're right.' He wasn't too sure about that, but didn't want to put a damper on proceedings.

The walk to the cliff face took longer than he expected, the distance being deceptive because of the openness, except for the piles of stones, each one a memorial to an attempt to breach the defences of the cliff dwellers, whoever they were.

'It might be a good idea for you to rest a while and take some food and water, as we do not know when we can rest again if we enter the cliff.'

'That suits me.' said a grateful Cresswell, sitting down on a convenient lump of rock.

Various vehicles went purposefully to and fro from the cave entrance, bent on some mission or other, but where they went or why was just as much a mystery as was the whole set-up of the mechanicals.

Feeling rested and refreshed, Cresswell arose to his feet, intrigued by what might lay ahead, but fearful that something might think him an interloper, and take the necessary action.

Carefully edging his way up to the entrance, Cresswell peered into the dark hole, and was surprised to see faint lights along the walls, and a walkway half a metre up from the floor level along one side of the tunnel.

'I think we should use that raised path, as I have seen no mechanicals use it so far.'

'OK, I'll climb up and see what it's like.'

The ledge was covered in dust, and it was obvious that it hadn't been used by anything for a very long time.

'Seems you're right, nothing has disturbed this dust for ages, so we should be all right.' Cresswell then realized that he had used the 'we' form for the first time intentionally, and felt better for acknowledging his companion's presence.

Slowly his eyes got used to the dim light, and Cresswell increased his pace as he went deeper into the tunnel complex.

He had been tramping on for some minutes when he came to the first of the office blocks, or that was what he thought they were.

Rooms had been cut out from the living rock, fronted with thick quartz glass through which he could only just see, and furnished with all the trappings he was used to seeing back on the smelter station.

The doors wouldn't open, try as he might, so he assumed that they were locked in some fashion, although he couldn't see how it was done.

There was no sign of any human beings or even a skeleton to decorate the otherwise austere surroundings, just the equipment in neat orderly rows, the chairs on which the builders of the place must have sat, and the thick dust to remind him that they had all left a long time ago.

Several other blocks of rooms were spaced along the tunnel before it opened out into a major highway junction, branches going off in all directions.

'I suppose the machines don't need signposts or directions.'

'True. They will all be programmed with their duties and where everything is located, I doubt if they can even see as we think of the term, although the dim lights do suggest that some form of guidance system is used.'

'Which way do we go now?' asked Cresswell, all routes looking the same to him.

'Stick to this ledge and follow it into the next section, if nothing interesting is found then we can return and go down the next one, so missing nothing.'

'Hey, it's my legs we're using.' He was almost sure he felt a mental grin from Vax.

The chosen tunnel proved to be the correct one for what they wanted to see. It opened out into a vast hall, the end of which disappeared into the hazy distance, a faint pall of dust and smoke hung in the air, masking the ability to see fine detail on the ground below them.

In the middle of the hall, a huge machine was under construction, dozens of little robots scurrying about carrying materials and tools, passing them on to others and then going back somewhere for more.

Larger machines riveted and bent sheets of metal, some cut with huge grinding wheels, sending great showers of sparks into the air adding lurid splashes of light to the place.

'What do you think they're building?' asked Cresswell, unable to see any fine detail through the dust haze.

'It looks like a vehicle intended to carry a large projectile launcher, I can just see the mounting for the tube. It is certainly the biggest machine we have seen yet. I do not think I would like to be on the receiving end of whatever it launches. Let us try one of the other tunnels.'

Going back to the main junction, Cresswell jumped down to the main trackway when there were no vehicles passing, climbed up onto the path which led into the next tunnel.

He had to go in some way before anything interesting came to light, and was surprised when it did. It resembled a chemistry laboratory, but not the kind he was used to.

Huge vats lined the walls, quartz crucibles and retorts were stacked along deep shelves for as far as he could see, while side tunnels led off every few metres into what he supposed would be store rooms.

Going along the ledge a little further, he came to an opening in the wall which led to one of the side rooms.

Cresswell peered in and saw what almost looked like a human being filling a long cylinder with powder from a pipe which hung down from the ceiling.

'Not a bad imitation I suppose, but why make a robot device in human style?'

'Mainly because it is a most efficient form for what it is doing. Consider, two legs for mobility with auto balance, two arms for manipulation, a high placed observation unit for assessing what is being done. Can you better that?'

'See what you mean, hadn't thought of it that way.'

Cresswell watched fascinated at the smooth efficiency of the robot figure as it went about the task of loading many long tubes with what he thought might be propellant for a missile.

'Let us move on a little, there is much to see.'

After viewing several more workshops involved in the various stages of missile manufacture, Vax sensed that something wasn't quite right, and this was later confirmed when the lighting system began to flicker in such a way as to suggest that a message was being transmitted via the rapidly blinking lights.

'The sequence of light pulses are being repeated at regular intervals, so I would assume that it must be a warning of some kind, possibly an attack, and therefore I think we should vacate the cave system as rapidly as possible.'

Cresswell also picked up the feeling that all wasn't well with the underground war factory, and turning on his heel began to run back the way they had come as fast as he could in the dim light.

'Slow down, or you will burn out your energy reserves, you may need to make an emergency sprint later on. I will guide you back along the ledges to the exit as I think there are a few short cuts we can make.'

Cresswell pounded on, only pausing when they had to cross over the tunnel roadway below the ledges to gain the ledges on the other side, as directed by Vax.

The amount of robot traffic was increasing all the time, and crossing the lower levels was becoming hazardous as the speed at which the little mobiles moved had risen greatly.

After what seemed like hours to Cresswell, they finally saw the glow of daylight up ahead, but had to wait for several minutes in order to safely cross over the track way onto the ledge on the other side for the final sprint to the outside.

'Turn to your right and go up that slope to the top. From there we should be out of the way of any attacking force and get a good view of what is about to happen.'

By the time Cresswell had reached the top of the rise in the ground indicated by Vax, he was totally out of breath and gasping for air to fill his aching lungs.

'That must have been the longest continuous run I have ever done in my entire long miss spent life.' he finally managed to gasp out.

'You did well. I have noticed that your body is responding to the extra exercise you have been doing of late, and it is getting very fit. We should be safe enough up here, and we have a very good view of the cave entrance and the big defence ditch to your right.'

As Cresswell turned to look in the direction of the ditch, he saw a small plume of dirty grey smoke rising up into the air over the slope beyond the huge trench.

'Looks like something is coming this way, could be the attacking force which initiated all the commotion below.'

They didn't have long to wait before the reason for the panic stricken mobilization became apparent. Over the brow of the slope beyond the defence ditch there hove into sight a massive machine, belching smoke and sparks from a huge exhaust chimney.

As it drew up to the edge of the ditch the smoke lessened a little, and it shuddered to a halt. Two smaller machines swept around from behind the monster and approached the ditch, positioning themselves very carefully before winching up a bridge section from a trailer like device each of them had been towing.

The two bridge sections swept majestically up and then gracefully lowered themselves down to the other side of the ditch, sending up a small cloud of dust and stones, and completing a way across the defences for the larger machine.

A phalanx of small defending robots had lined themselves up opposite the bridge, and two of them slowly advanced towards the new threat to their domain.

A huge plume of smoke and sparks belched forth from the stack on the giant machine, which had been patiently waiting for the bridge to be completed. Slowly it edged forward, aligning itself carefully with the bridge sections, and then proceeded to lumber across the defence trench.

The two defence robots, which by now had also gained a footing on the opposite side of the bridge, fired off their armaments at the approaching giant.

The shells exploded harmlessly against the massive solid steel shielding on the front of the machine, and it edged slowly forward, the bridge dipping slightly under the strain of such a colossal load.

The two defence robots were crushed flat as the giant approached the other side of the trench, and a furious fusillade of shells from the defenders splattered harmlessly against it as it gained the solid ground beyond the bridge.

The defender robots rallied round to try and block the way of the giant machine, but were brushed aside as were the piles of stone blocks which also stood in its path.

Other fighting machines were now emerging from the cave entrance and discharged their weapons towards the approaching monster, but nothing seemed to deter it from its intent to reach the cliff entrance.

'That machine is far too big to go into the cave, so what do you think it will do?' asked Cresswell, totally overwhelmed by the sheer ferocity of the conflict.

'I do not think the machine intends to go into the cave system itself, but something else might well do so. We shall soon see as nothing seems

able to stop it.'

About twenty metres from the cave entrance the big machine stopped, and Cresswell waited with bated breath to see what would happen next.

The huge steel shutter on the front of the attacker slowly rose upwards, revealing another smaller and squatter device hidden beneath. This new robot, equipped with tracks, slowly edged forwards, and then with a blast of black smoke from its exhaust, raced into the tunnel dragging a long length of flexible pipe behind it which was being fed off a large drum on the main machine.

'Good god, it's going in for hundreds of metres.' exclaimed Cresswell, hardly able to believe his eyes.

At last the end of the flexible pipe must have been reached, for it stopped wriggling about on the ground, and all was still, for a while.

The next thing Cresswell knew was a deep shudder in the ground beneath him and a concussion wave which knocked him off his feet.

A monstrous jet of angry red flames spewed out of the cave entrance, engulfing the attacking machine from end to end, followed by boiling clouds of black and brown smoke and not a few sparks.

The whole cliff face seemed to heave itself up several metres and then crashed down in a torrent of smashed rock and earth, covering the still flaming attacker and all the small defending robots which had closed in around it.

By the time he had got to his feet, and his ears had stopped ringing, all was quiet again with just the odd rumble of a piece of rock settling down in its new position. A few wisps of smoke seeped out from cracks along the cliff face along with a little dust, but that too soon disappeared, leaving the scene as tranquil as it had been hours before.

'There's no way we can get back into the cave factory now, not that there's any real point in doing so, but a look at the other side who mounted the attack might be informative.'

'I see no reason why we should not do so, if you think it would be of interest to you, but I do not think I would gain much from it.'

'Well, let's just have a brief look to see if they operate any differently.'

Cresswell made his way back to the defence trench and gingerly climbed up onto the girder structure used by the big attacking machine.

It had been only just strong enough, as the middle section was badly bent, and another few tens of kilos might well have sent the whole thing crashing down to the watery depths below.

It was only when he was halfway across that he realized just how high above the water he was, and despite his experiences in outer space, he didn't like the sensation. This was a new kind of vertigo.

Gaining the other side, it was easy to follow the trail left by the big machine, and by late afternoon, having not found the other group, Cresswell called a halt.

'You would be wise to take food and rest for a time, I will keep a lookout for anything I consider to be threatening, so rest well.'

And rest he did. Odd dreams of strange machines filled his sleeping hours, and when he did finally awake, he was eager to tell Vax about them.

'They are of no consequence. They are merely pictures in your mind, some of real events, some manufactured to fit the sequence and strung together to amuse you while your body takes a rest and repairs itself.'

'Oh.' was all he could say to that.

It took two more days of walking before Cresswell came to what he thought might be the enemy's stronghold, and then he wasn't too sure.

The track made by the big machine ended on a rocky ledge, leaving white powder marks where the hard steel tracks had cut into the rock surface, and they just stopped right at the very end of the huge stone slab overhanging the valley below.

Peering over the edge, Cresswell had another of those unpleasant feelings he had experienced on the girder bridge, and backed away from the sheer drop of several hundred metres to the valley below.

'I do not understand. You feel a dreadful fear of a short drop like that, and yet you did not feel so when out in space which was much more threatening I would have thought.'

'I can't explain it either. Never did like heights, but space never worries me much.'

Not wishing to discuss his irrational fears any further, Cresswell walked around the ledge, looking for any signs which would explain how the big machine had got here without leaving any tracks, but could find nothing.

'Those marks go right to the edge, it can't have flown in, so how did it get here?'

'I do not know. Perhaps if we wait a while something else might use the same route, and then we shall know.'

'I'm going to take another look over that ledge, keep an eye on me to make sure I don't do anything silly.'

Cresswell crawled right up to the lip, and looked over, straining his eyes to see what lay at the bottom of the drop.

'Now that's interesting, there's a small collection of machines, all battered to bits, lying down there.

I'll bet this ledge is a trap for their enemies. They somehow entice the others out here and they go chasing the tracks, and before you know it, there're over the edge.'

'That is possible, but I would think there is something more to it than that. Let us look for other tracks, there may be some.'

While Cresswell was idly looking at an old tree stump he made the discovery that they were possibly being observed.

'That old stump isn't what it looks like, I'm sure I saw it move just now.'

He went over to the remains of the shattered tree, and casually walking around it, reached out and gave the trunk a hard thump with his clenched fist.

'It sounds hollow, now that's not natural, surely.'

Climbing onto a nearby rock, he could look directly down on the top end of the stump, and saw a small shiny window set in its side near the top.

'It looks like a periscope, a device for viewing something when you are below the ground or whatever, I saw something like it on an old data tape once.'

'What we need is something metallic which we can move around to stimulate the looking device into action, I do not think it is programmed to locate us.'

Search as they might, there was nothing metallic in the vicinity, and a trip down to the bottom of the cliff to retrieve something from the wrecked robots was too arduous to even contemplate.

'If you can climb up and cover the eye of the viewer that should provoke some action, as it would register as a fault in the system, or some outside interference.'

'Oh, I like that! Good thinking.' Cresswell's sense of humour was coming back again.

There was little out on the barren ground to make a cover with, but eventually Cresswell found some pieces of bark and a few strands of dried grass.

After giving Vax a few new words to query at a later date, he managed to fashion a crude cover to slip over the eye of the viewer, but it was too high for him to reach and he didn't like the idea of trying to climb up the trunk.

A small branch which had survived the grinding action of the many tracked vehicles which had passed this way solved the problem, and Cresswell did a very good imitation of a distraught ballet dancer on tip toes in his efforts to slip the bark cover over the lens.

'Well, that should do it. I'll bet 'they' think its night time all of a sudden.'

'I would suspect that the device also works in the infra red band, so night and day would be the same, but it should elicit a response.'

And it did. Cresswell could feel a low vibration through his feet, and a deep rumbling noise from under the ground.

He jumped back just in time as a section of the rocky ledge he was standing on began it's decent to the depths below.

As he was about to peer over the edge, the rock platform hove into view again, and on it stood the weirdest little robot they had yet encountered.

Three sets of rotating tracks formed a tripod system giving great stability to the otherwise ungainly looking creation. Attached to the main body were a selection of jointed arms, each equipped with a different type of tool, but what they were for could only be guessed at as they made little sense.

When the platform had reached ground level again, the little robot trundled forward and made its way up to the viewing tree.

One by one the arms flexed and wove a strange pattern in the air, as though the robot was confused at what it saw and couldn't make its mind up as to which tool to use. After much clanking and rattling, one arm extended itself and grasped the bark covering on top of the viewing tree, and then lifted it clear.

The tree then rotated it's viewing eye through a full circle, as if testing the view wasn't being obstructed by anything else, and the little robot, having received a signal that all was well, turned and rattled it's way back to the rock platform it had come up on.

'If you wish to go below, you had better get onto the platform now.'

Although feeling a bit uneasy, Cresswell joined the robot, standing just behind it as the platform began it's decent.

'Notice how the platform not only goes down, but is travelling at a forty five degree angle with respect to the cliff face, and is retreating into the body of the cliff. This would account for the tracks on the other platform going right up to the edge of the platform.'

Cresswell said 'yes', but wasn't quite sure if he understood just what was implied.

As they went lower, a faint light, similar to that in the other factory which had been destroyed, bathed the platform as it descended. With a deep thump, the platform reached the bottom of its travel, and the robot began moving off.

He trotted along behind it for a few metres until it reached a section of the tunnel which sported a single rail in its centre. The robot adjusted its pair of forward tracks to climb onto a small flat topped truck which sat on top of the rail, and the truck then began to move along the track.

'Quick, jump onto the platform, unless you want a possibly very long walk.'

There was just enough room for the two of them, Cresswell holding on uneasily to the now stationary robot as the platform gathered speed until the tunnel sides were a blur.

There were many branch tunnels, and a points system sent the platform rattling and clanking along a predetermined route, the sudden changes of direction almost shaking Cresswell from his precarious position next to the robot, which seemed to be rooted to the platform itself.

With a final squeal and clank, the platform stopped and the robot trundled off to place itself into a niche in the tunnel wall.

Cresswell also jumped down as the platform sped off into the distance, no doubt called to perform another duty somewhere else within the complex.

'Now where do we go?'

'That is up to you. We can not get lost as long as we follow the tracks and use the points system as arrows pointing towards the exit.'

Cresswell set off at a slow trot following the route taken by the departing platform, and wishing Vax was a little more enthusiastic about the exploration.

'One thing I don't understand is why the two warring factions are positioned so near to each other, unless of course, we landed smack bang between them and the nation states they represent.'

'I do not think it is likely, or that simple. I would suppose that in the beginning of the robot war there were many factories on each side, and once out of human control, and over a long period of time, each factory developed its own particular type of attacking devices which may not be recognized by the other factories as belonging to the side. Hence, each factory now attacks any other factory which uses a different type of robot to its own.'

'That means the war will continue until there's nothing left to make armaments with, and then they'll just batter each other with flailing arms.'

'*It would seem so.*'

'And there's nothing we can do about it?'

'*Not that I can see.*'

Cresswell trotted on in silence, there was little else to say.

The tunnel seemed endless, with offshoots delving ever deeper into the hillside from either side, and each one with its own monorail system.

'The air in here is a lot cleaner than the other place we visited, and there's a gentle breeze blowing through, I didn't know machines would appreciate clean air!'

'*I doubt that is the answer. Most likely it is a still functioning system put in by the humans, or possibly the machines have realized that dust could be detrimental to their manufacturing techniques.*'

'That smacks of intelligence, surely.'

'*Not in the sense of the word as you would use it. It is purely a device designed to observe all data, and then amend its actions to optimise productivity.*'

'Well, it seems bloody bright to me.' grumbled Cresswell, feeling put down again by his companion's superior knowledge and powers of deduction.

Several times Cresswell had to leap for the side wall of the tunnel as a speeding platform came whistling towards him, sometimes empty, sometimes loaded to a point of over spilling.

Having taken one of the side tunnels, he came to an open hall of immense proportions, the high vaulted ceiling almost out of sight in the faint haze above and stretching off into the distance for hundreds of metres.

In the centre of the first section, something vast had been constructed and moved on to another place, as was evident by the debris and odd pieces of cut metal lying about.

'I'll bet this was where the big attacker was built, but how did they get it out of here? Certainly not down the tunnel we came through.'

'*I think you are correct. The space left clear of debris is about the same size, and I would expect there to be another exit apart from the big lift.*'

'What big lift, did I miss something?'

'*The big ledge we found when we first came to this place, the one with the white tracks on it.*'

'You mean that's a lift? Good God, it must be colossal.'

'Look a little further down the hall, there is another machine under construction, let us go and have a look at it, there seem to be no robots around to cause a problem.'

Close up, Cresswell was almost overcome by the size of the monstrosity before him. It looked the same as the one which had attacked the cliff factory, but this close, the sheer immensity of it was more apparent.

Only partly complete, it looked as if it had been abandoned as news of the success of the first machine had come through, there being no need to waste materials on a machine which was no longer required.

The great drums which would hold the explosive fire mixture were in place as was the device to drag the flexible tubes deep into the target area. Cresswell wanted to see the mighty engine which would drive the colossus, but was hindered by the superstructure which would eventually carry the protective sheets.

'It looks as if there isn't a lot more to do to make this machine workable.'

'What do you have in mind?'

'Oh, nothing. Just wondered if we could get it going, I'd love to drive something as big as this.'

'I doubt if it is fuelled up, that would be done at the last moment because of the fire risk.'

Cresswell wandered around the hall, looking at several other smaller machines, but was unable to figure out just what they were intended to do upon completion.

'I think it is time we left this place. I am picking up something, but I do not know what it is.'

'Let's see if we can get out by the big lift you mentioned earlier, although God knows how we operate it.'

The end of the hall proved to be the exit point for the big machine, and Cresswell hurried along the wide tunnel which was equipped with two rails of massive proportions, leading, he hoped to the lift.

After he had been jogging along for some time, a deep rumbling sound echoed along the tunnel and he instinctively flung himself against the tunnel wall, and only just in time.

A platform of huge proportions thundered by, heading for the hall they had just left.

'Perhaps they're going to finish the other machine after all.'

'I do not think we should be around to see if they do, as that would

suppose that another threat was imminent.'

Cresswell hurried on, following the twin rails as if his life depended upon it. He too, could feel something was not quite right about the place.

The tunnel terminated in another hall, and this one contained the lift mechanism which had launched the big attacker.

A network of massive girders formed a sloping ramp down which the huge stone slab of the lift platform above would slide, if they could figure out how to use it.

'There doesn't seem to be any controls for it that I can see, maybe it's worked from somewhere else.'

'I think the controls would be local. Let us be systematic about this. They may not look like anything we are used to, as they are for a machine's use.'

Cresswell quartered the area around the base of the huge ramp, but there was nothing remotely like a control box, and he was about to give up when he felt his body stop.

'I think that might be it.' and he felt his head turn slightly to one side.

A small recess about half a metre from the floor level concealed a box-like structure with a hole in the middle.

The light was too dim to show much in the way of detail, but the hole obviously invited something to be put into it, and Cresswell wasn't about to offer his hand.

'We need a piece of rod-like material to operate this device I would think, I'll see if I can find something.'

But he didn't. The operators of the factory were meticulous in their tidiness.

'Now what do we do? There's nothing lying around here we can use. Shall I go back to the assembly hall and look for something there?'

Before he could get an answer, a deep rumbling noise echoed along the tunnel.

'I think we should get out of the way of the rails, something is coming.'

Seconds later the big platform came rushing up to the lift station, a squeal of metal on metal as it braked hard just short of the ramp.

On the platform was one of the flying machines they had seen earlier, with its rotors folded back neatly like a giant hand pointing back along the tunnel. A small three tracker rattled its way off the back of the platform and went over to the recess in the wall, extended a long probe like arm and inserted it into the hole in the box.

There was silence for a while, and a dismayed Cresswell thought the mechanism had broken down, but heaved a sigh of relief as a low grinding sound began to fill the hall, and a chink of light from the outside world filtered down from around the edge of the descending lift slab, illuminating a drift of dust and sand into a spangled shower of glittering particles.

'We must be ready to jump onto the platform as soon as the flying machine is loaded as I suspect there will be little hesitation before the lift goes up again.'

The great slab of stone finally reached the floor level, and sank into a recess so that the lift platform was level with the end of the twin tracks holding the transporter.

The smaller robot who had summoned the lift, returned to the transporter platform and began to push the flying machine onto the stone slab, and having got it into an approved position, trundled back to the transporter.

Cresswell leapt onto the slab, and holding onto a strut of the flying machine, began the journey up into the outside world.

To begin with, the stronger light hurt his eyes, and Vax must have felt the same as Cresswell's pupils contracted down to a pinpoint size causing a loss of clear vision for a few moments.

The platform of rock ground its way up the long ramp and eventually locked into place on the surrounding ledge.

Even as he jumped clear, the rotor blades of the flying machine began to unfurl and the sound of a rather rough engine starting up split the otherwise still air.

Clouds of blue smoke enveloped the scene for a few moments as the engine cleared its oily throat, and then the blades began to whirr and rattle.

The ensuing blast of air sent him flying and cursing as the great machine lumbered into the air, turned to face the valley below, and then sped off on some unknown mission.

'By the number of tubes and blobs slung under its belly, someone is going to get a pasting.' Cresswell commented.

'I think we should clear the area in case there is some retaliation from the recipient of that conglomeration of armament, I do not suppose they will be very pleased to receive it.'

He wound his way back down the hillside to the plain below, stopping every now and again to see if the hill had disgorged any more robots, and in so doing nearly fell over one.

A round ball, nearly half a metre in diameter, sat on a frame attached to a pair of tracks, a large glass eye mounted on a flexible arm surveying the astonished Cresswell.

Suddenly it came to life, scuttling backwards until it hit a rock, and then skidded around it to continue to glare at the strange apparition on two legs.

The arm with the lens waved up and down, and then sideways, taking in a good all round picture of Cresswell and the surrounding scenery, no doubt trying to decide if he was part of the local area, or something which had to be investigated.

A soft whirring sound accompanied the extrusion of an aerial from the back of the robot as it continued to stare at Cresswell.

'Quick, bend or break that rod, it is going to transmit some sort of signal announcing our presence.'

He sprinted the short distance between them and flung himself forward on top of the robot, grabbing the aerial in both hands and putting all his weight behind the thrust, bending it down until it touched the ground.

'Wrench it out of its hole if you can.'

Cresswell tried, but the steel rod was firmly anchored to something within the body, and it wouldn't come out.

He did the next best thing by twisting the thin rod around until he had jammed it between one of the caterpillar tracks, then the robot suddenly sprang to life and raced around in a tight circle as the jammed track refused to rotate.

Realizing that the robot had to be destroyed before it could send back to its base knowledge of their presence, he picked up as large a rock as he could, and repeatedly slammed it onto the other caterpillar track.

This much onslaught from a solid lump of rock was more than the design features of the robot had allowed for, and the track finally split, the drive wheels sending it scurrying along the ground with a life of its own.

Cresswell then concentrated on the main body of the machine, eventually managing to split it open to display a complicated arrangement of electronics, but before he could study the entrails of the robot, the main storage battery short circuited in a blaze of blue and white sparks, discharging its energy in one fearful pulse, melting the surrounding metal and reducing the unit to a worthless pile of junk metal.

He was surprised that he didn't feel pleased with his achievement, a certain sadness at having destroyed something which was defenceless being the main cause, but then, it had to be done in case the robot initiated an attack from something a lot bigger.

'You did well there. A pity we could not have had a look at the inside of it though, we may have learned something about the technical level of these devices.'

'They're quite technical enough for me.' rejoined Cresswell, panting from his exertions.

'Do you think it got its radio message off?'

'We have no way of knowing, unless we stay here for a while, and I would suggest we do not give that option any thought.'

Cresswell continued on down the hill, glancing over his shoulder every once in a while to make sure they were not followed.

A small stream trickled down through the boulders at the point where the hill blended into the plain, and he paused for a drink of fresh water, filling his water containers at the same time.

Having slaked his thirst, he then reconstituted one of his food concentrate blocks, wishing he had something a little tastier to hand, and looking forward to the day when he could get back to a more civilized form of eating.

His reverie was broken by the twack-twack of rotor blades in the distance, and glancing up he could see what he thought was the flying machine returning to its base.

As the craft drew nearer it was plain to see that it had been attacked by something, the rotor blades were not sounding as even in their gyrations as they had been and a small stream of smoke or fuel could be seen trailing behind.

As it came in to land, several smaller dots came into view on the horizon, growing bigger by the moment. From his position on the plain, Cresswell couldn't see the actual lowering of the flying machine into the lift shaft, but the hill looked as naked as it had before, as the first of the new flying machines drew near.

The distant dots had grown into long sleek missiles as they roared up the valley, one peeling off as the others circled around as if looking for a target.

The loner went back down the length of the valley, suddenly climbing vertically and flipping over, to come streaking back under full power, aiming as far as he could tell, for the face of the cliff containing the factory they had not long left.

An ear shattering roar followed a blinding flash of light as the missile struck the cliff, sending thousands of tonnes of rock crashing down to the valley below, the thunder of its falling echoing on for several minutes.

The other missiles continued to circle until the dust had cleared a little, and then the next one peeled off from the circle, streaked up the valley and returned to deliver another stunning blow to the already battered cliff.

'The flying machine must have upset someone rather badly.' Cresswell managed to get out between explosions and dodging the odd piece of rock which came whistling down from above.

The last missile delivered its warhead through the ever deepening hole punched in the cliff face by its predecessors, and the ensuing gout of flame signalled that it had penetrated deep into the complex, and had probably struck a fuel or explosive store.

The whole hill heaved itself up, and then settled down amid a vast cloud of dust and debris, the factory totally destroyed, and another contestant out of the game.

'That's two warring factory units knocked out in the short time we've been here, surely there can't be much left after a year or so?'

'It could be just coincidence that these two units happened to annihilate each other in such a short space of time. But the war will go on for some time to come, I would think. You now have a greater distance between units, so they have a chance to grow and develop more sophisticated weaponry, and because of the increased distance between them, will have to develop longer range weapons. I think your mother world will be senselessly ploughed up for some time to come, sadly.'

Cresswell instinctively knew there was no place for him on earth, unless he could find one of his dreamed of desert islands, but then he would have the difficulty of getting supplies, and as for getting there, wherever there was, he didn't think he stood a chance.

'I think it would be as well to return to the shuttle, just in case something has found it, and decided to convert the metalwork into something more to its liking.'

'Yes, I think you're right, there's nothing for me here. It doesn't look as if there will be peace in my lifetime, and how will I survive when the concentrates run out? I won't, is the short answer.'

He dusted himself off, re-stowed his belongings, such as they were, and set off across the plain in the direction he thought the shuttle would be in.

A grassy area broke the monotony of the otherwise barren sand

and churned up earth, and Cresswell felt somewhat cheered up by the bright green of the new shoots which had, against all odds, taken a firm hold on the landscape. A few small bushes had escaped the withering blast of the warring robots, and almost amounted to a wooded area.

'I think I'll take a break here, it looks peaceful enough and my legs could do with a rest.' and so saying, he sat down under the shade of the largest patch of greenery he had yet seen since arriving on his home world.

'You know, I used to see areas like this while watching the old history programs on the vision displays, but I never thought I'd actually sit in one.'

'You mean they did not exist at that time?'

'I expect they existed somewhere, but we never got to see them, the whole damn place was too crowded with people.

'You've no idea just how many people there were, and they all had to be housed and supplied with the trappings of life.'

'I had wondered if your people had population control, it would seem they did not think it was necessary.'

'Oh it was necessary all right, but no one was going to be the first to do it, so it didn't get done. We just overran the earth until all possible spaces which could be used, were used, and then we began fighting over the less habitable parts, rendering them even less habitable. That's the main reason for my taking to space and the asteroid run. Just to get away from this God awful mess.'

Cresswell lay back on the grass between the little trees, shut his eyes and drank in the refreshing smell of the new greenery. This was more like the kind of life he would liked to have lived, but this was only a short respite before facing up to the realities of that which now existed.

The very faint chink and scrape of metal on metal brought him wide awake again.

'I thought it was too good to be true.'

'It would seem likely that there is something mechanical occurring beyond your haven of trees, and I think we should find out what it is in case we have to avoid it.'

Cresswell, feeling a little annoyed at having his dream shattered yet again, arose to his feet and carefully, so as not to damage too much of the grass, made his way through the wood and out onto the plain beyond.

A small ridge gave him the necessary cover to get a little closer to the source of the metallic sounds, and he dropped down to ground level to crawl the last few metres.

Peering over the ridge of stones he could see two small robots happily hacking away at what remained of a much larger one, which had failed or been disabled at some time, and they were bent on salvaging all that was possible.

There was nothing sophisticated about the way they went about this. A small cutting flame sliced the main covering up into manageable pieces, which were then lifted onto what looked like a trailer, while the other one seemed to specialize in removing the units exposed by the flame cutter by giving them a hefty jerk.

'I do not think they will be interested in us, but to be on the safe side, let us return to the wooded area, and go around them.'

Somehow the wood didn't seem quite so enticing when he went through it again, so Cresswell marched on towards the area on the plain where his shuttle lay.

Not all the streams he came across were fit for drinking. Some were heavily laden with silt, no doubt churned up by a procession of wandering robots, while others had a distinct metallic flavour as if they had drained out from an old mine working, or been tainted by some poor robot quietly decomposing in its watery grave.

But generally he managed to find enough potable supplies to keep him from dying from thirst, so that was the least of his worries.

Several times a flying machine droned overhead, and a tank-like vehicle was seen ploughing its way along the brow of an adjacent hill, leaving behind a thin trail of blue smoke which gradually broke up and dissipated in the now still air.

Cresswell was beginning to wonder if he was heading in the correct direction, when cresting a low ridge the shuttle could be clearly seen in the far distance like a gleaming silver bullet.

He had covered about half the distance to the shuttle when Vax interrupted his otherwise semi dream like state as he marched along.

'Look over there on that rise, there is a robot standing guard on the shuttle.'

'How do you know that, it might just be standing there admiring the view.' Cresswell was in a flippant mood now that the shuttle was so close.

'Because it is pointing in that direction and has an aerial extended, possibly sending messages or directing others to this place. I think we should disable it, and then make haste to the shuttle.'

'I'll try and creep up on it from behind and then give it the old stone treatment.'

'Disable the aerial first, we do not want it telling others that an attack has occurred.'

Cresswell was almost pleased to have something to do other than just walk, and he felt his adrenaline level go up a couple of notches as he made his way up the slope towards the back of the unsuspecting robot.

Two metres from his quarry and the robot emitted a low whirring noise and began to turn on its tracks.

Cresswell hurled himself forward. Jumping onto the back of the machine and reaching up as high as he could, he grabbed the aerial with both hands and jumped down again, dragging the aerial with him and hearing a healthy snap as it broke away from its base.

Remembering his success the last time he had disabled a robot, he quickly jammed the broken off aerial in between the tracks on one side of the machine and then looked around for a suitable rock to effect the coup de grace.

The robot was still powered up, and as it could only use one of its tracks, it spun around knocking Cresswell flying, and nearly ran over his foot.

With yet another new word for Vax to query, he staggered to his feet, picked up a piece of rock and rammed it between the spinning tracks and the drive wheels of the machine the next time it came around.

The high pitched whine of the drive unit rose to an even higher pitched scream, and then stopped, a thin wisp of smoke seeping out from the rear end of the robot.

Once again all was still as the dust settled, the smoke drifted away, and Cresswell sat down on the now defunct machine to get his breath back.

'I do think we should get down to the shuttle as soon as possible, but before we do, it might be a good idea to get the robot out of sight. If you remove some of the stones from the other side of it, you may be able to tip it over and roll it down the hill where it will be out of direct line of sight of any others coming this way.'

Cresswell got up and tried his best, but some of the stones were large, heavy and bedded in. The robot was at an angle anyway, so he though it shouldn't take too much of a push to get moving down the slope. But it did.

He heaved and strained, but all he could do was to cause it to rock a little. Suddenly, he felt his body stiffen, the muscles flex, and with a great surge the robot was over on its side and rolling down the hill in a slither of lose stones and dirt to disappear into a small ravine.

'Thanks for that. Pity it's me who will have the sore muscles afterwards though.'

'I shall feel it too. I am sorry, I felt it necessary.'

It's OK, I'm just being a little churlish at not being able to do it myself.'

'But you could have, it is only a matter of sending the correct messages to the right muscles, normally you only use about one third of the power available in your body.'

He set off down the slope towards the distant shuttle, not daring to mentally mutter to himself what he would have liked to, as he knew his companion would be listening in and would probably get the wrong idea or not understand his view point at all.

'Do you think you could increase your pace a little, there is a line of mechanicals heading towards the shuttle.'

Cresswell looked over his shoulder to see five or six robots of varying sizes racing down a far slope with sparks coming from their tracks as they bit into the stony ground, and a plume of dust trailing behind them.

It was all he needed to make a super human effort, and by the time he had reached the shuttle he was fighting for breath, the air whistling in and out of his parched throat like a leaky pair of bellows.

He grasped the thin cord down which he had shinned when he had left the shuttle, but try as he might, he couldn't get sufficient grip on it to haul himself up.

Once again, he felt his body being taken over, and the arms working like steam driven pistons, his body dangling below but ascending at a prodigious rate.

Reaching the partly open hatch, he hauled himself in, dragging the cord in behind him and slammed the hatch shut all in one smooth action.

Cresswell headed for the forward control cabin, sat down in the pilot's seat and promptly went to pieces.

'I can't remember what does what for God's sake.' tears of frustration beginning to flow down his face.

'Do not worry, I will fly the shuttle, leave it to me.'

Cresswell watched with a strange feeling of detachment as his body settled itself down at the controls, his hands flying over various buttons and knobs in a fluid graceful motion.

The main power unit came on with a thunderous roar, the side thrusters turning the shuttle around to face the way they had come in to land, and then he felt his body being thrust back into the seat with a force which frightened him.

A vast fan shaped column of dust and small stones streamed out behind the shuttle as it accelerated across the plain, with the odd bone jarring thump as one of the wheels hit a stone which it couldn't cope with.

Finally the nose lifted, and the only sound left was the scream of cleaved air and the deep throated roar of the main drive as they gained height, the land slipping away below.

Gradually Cresswell's eyes regained their focus and he felt in control once again, not that he really minded Vax taking over as he was sure he couldn't have made such a perfect take off unaided.

'*I suggest we cruise at this height for a while to see if there is any land which is not as devastated as that which we have just left. There should be the odd pockets here and there.*'

Five:
Ashes and Rock

'THAT'S FINE BY me, but will we have enough fuel to leave the planet and get up into orbit with the smelter station?'

'*Yes, I think so. We used very little on the way down, and the fuel gauge has hardly moved from the position it was in when we left the smelter station.*'

They flew on beneath leaden skies with the occasional break as a weak sun broke through. The power unit having reduced its roar to a gentle murmur, there was only the whistling rush of air and the changing landscape below to indicate that they were in motion.

A range of mountains slid by beneath them, the once majestic dark green forests reduced to a field of grey ash with the occasional blackened tree stump poking through.

Even the normally pristine sparkling white snow on the mountains had a grey tinge to it from the high level fine ash fallout, adding a dull and dismal touch to the overall picture.

'How could we have done this to such a beautiful planet?' Cresswell asked, feeling the sting of salt tears at the back of his eyes.

For once Vax thought it better to say nothing as his partner tried to come to terms with what he had seen.

The shuttle flew on, crossing a vast plain of churned up earth and rock with very little vegetation to break the grey and brown monotony, except for several enormous shallow depressions where atomics had been used, rendering all life impossible for countless aeons of time to come.

A large conurbation on the coast had been reduced to a twisted mass of steel girders and smashed concrete, a totally bare patch in the middle where the epicentre of the blast had melted everything and left a rippled glassy circular patch partly filled with radioactive water.

They crossed a dull grey green sea which seemed to reluctantly heave itself into some sort of motion, the heavy oily swell only just discernible, the waves more like ripples.

A smudge on the horizon heralded another coastline, and Cresswell leaned forward eagerly to see what it would disclose, hoping against hope for some sign that all civilization as he had known it hadn't perished.

The shuttle sped across the divide between water and land only to be greeted by several fire tailed missiles rising up.

Vax immediately took over the controls and lifted the shuttle out of range, the missiles dropping back to earth with their propellant spent, to gouge out yet another series of craters.

'It doesn't look much different here.' commented Cresswell, disappointment clearly showing in his voice.

'There may well be small pockets of land which have escaped the devastation, and life there should carry on, although the radiation will have a mutating effect on it in time. Perhaps a new species will emerge, better able to survive in these conditions.'

'Can we reach the polar regions with the fuel we have left and still have enough to get back into space?'

'I would think so, we do not use up much cruising at this speed.'

The shuttle turned south, following the long eastern coastline of the Americas, crossing the Gulf of Mexico and all the way down to the southern-most tip of what was once Argentina.

A few minutes later the great ice cap of Antarctica could be seen on the horizon, but as they dropped a little lower to get a clearer view, it was obvious that all wasn't well with this last haven of mankind.

The Ross Ice Shelf had completely disappeared, and a massive rift had formed allowing the Ross sea to connect up with the Weddell, Graham Land having vanished as though it had never been.

The area of sea around what was left of the great ice cap was littered with massive icebergs for many kilometres out from it's riven shores, and great areas which were once covered in ice, now showing a dirty brown or black as the glaciers either slipped or melted to join the immense flotilla of jostling icebergs around the coastline.

'And to think for generations we had agreements protecting Antarctica from this sort of thing, and now it's all ruined.' Cresswell was as angry as he could ever recall being.

'I am very sorry for you and your people, it must have been a beautiful place.'

'It was, it was. The whole lot will melt now. It's been in a very delicate state of balance for thousands of years, the sea currents flowing around it preventing a big melt down, but now there is nothing to stop the whole bloody lot from melting, and that will submerge most of the low lying coastal lands all over earth. The changes in weather due to the melt down was what most people feared, but that doesn't matter now, there's no one left to complain.

'I wouldn't mind betting the same thing has happened to the North

Pole, God what a mess. I don't think there's any point in us hanging around on earth any more, there's nothing here for me now, we may as well get back to the smelter station, at least we'll have provisions to last out my lifetime up there.'

'I agree with that. Again, I am so very sorry.'

The power unit's tone rose several octaves and the shuttle's nose came up, the long journey spiralling up to the smelter station had begun.

Many times it was to encircle the earth, each time gaining height until it was virtually free of the planet's gravity, and the long curving sweep up towards the smelter station began.

'The other smelters are almost in the same orbit as ours, why not take a look at them to see what's happened to the opposition?'

'I see no reason why not, we have the fuel to do that.'

As the first of the smelters to come into view it left no doubt in Cresswell's mind that it was no accident which had befallen them. The great reflector arrays were a tangled mass of spidery girders, draped with their reflective coverings in ripped shreds. The main station had a huge section blown out of it and must have decompressed in seconds, killing all the crew in one fell swoop.

As the shuttle slipped by they could see the ferocity of the attack which must have occurred, several gaping holes in the outer skin showed where high speed missiles had penetrated the outer sheathing and exploded inside, ballooning the structure outwards like a series of giant boils. Nothing could have survived the attack, and Cresswell decided there was little point in trying to board the station to salvage anything as it probably would have been ripped to shreds along with its occupants.

'I would assume the other station has suffered the same fate, but we could take a look at it on the way around just in case there is anything you can salvage.'

The second station, when it was passed, had indeed been decimated, systematically ripped apart in wanton destruction, just a tangled mess of wreckage slowly twisting in space to mark one of man's greatest achievements and a perfect demonstration of his extreme folly.

'It is all so pointless, I just can't believe it has happened. Everything man has ever done, wiped out in one fell swoop.'

'It has happened before, on other worlds, and life in one form or another has survived. All is not lost, although from your view point, I can understand the terrible frustration and sense of loss you must be

feeling.'

'You mean there are other idiots out there, tearing each other apart?'

'Yes, many. But not all of them go down the same path as your people. Some learn as they go along, others do not. Rest assured, life goes on, something will be salvaged from the wreckage of your world, and in time it may even attain an intelligent state, and begin the game all over again.'

'Although I shan't see it, I hope they get it right next time.'

The shuttle cruised on, leaving the tattered remains of the Asian station to the fates of space, and then Cresswell's station came into view.

'Have you considered what to do next?'

'Restock the tug so that I can survive a little longer, but after that what else is there to do? I haven't lost the will to live, but what am I going to live for? Rock collecting is pointless. The tug can't leave the solar system, it's just not designed for that kind of travel. There's no place on earth which looked habitable, so it's you, me, and the tug. I suppose we could just park it in orbit, and look at the stars.'

'I would suggest that you restock and refuel the tug, and then we could go out to the asteroid belt, there are many things out there of interest, I am sure.'

'Such as?' Cresswell had never felt so despondent.

'The other alien ship for a start. Where did it go with us, could we make it go on that journey again? Are there other ships out there? What was the asteroid belt before it became so? I am sure once you accept the facts as they are, you will find your interest in life rekindled.'

'I suppose you're right, you usually are. I don't mean that in an unpleasant manner, but you seem to have been one step ahead of me just about every time we hit a crisis.'

'That may be so, but do not forget, my survival depends upon you surviving as well, so my motives are a little selfish in actual fact.'

Cresswell couldn't argue with that, so he brought the shuttle into a parking orbit with the smelter station and prepared to leave it for the last time.

Dragging the necessary food concentrates and other supplies from the stores to the exit hatch next to parked tug, was harder work and took a lot longer than he thought, so he took several breaks to explore the station to break up the monotony of the job.

One section of the station seemed to have sustained little damage from the attack, and Cresswell managed to force his way into the store rooms where the reclaimed minerals were kept prior to their despatch to earth.

Row upon row of shelves were stocked with bars of precious metals, the value of which nearly blew his mind.

'Just look at this! I've never seen so much potential wealth. You could have bought earth over and over again with this lot. Why would they stockpile so much up here when it was so needed down there?'

'*I would suspect it was what you would refer to as maximizing the market, holding stocks until the highest price for the materials could be achieved, and probably causing a shortage of the materials in the first place in order to do so.*'

'My God, you've got us humans taped!'

'*We have been watching your people for a long time, ever since your first attempts at space travel, so we have learnt much, although we do not always understand all of it.*'

Another store room was full of precious and semiprecious gem stones, extracted from the mineral rocks which had been brought into the station for smelting, and Cresswell helped himself to a good selection for working on later.

Something drew him to one corner of the store room, and there on a shelf all by itself was a box containing three long hexagonal deep purple crystals of outstanding beauty.

'I've never seen anything like these before, do you recognize them?'

'*Yes, but only from description, I have never actually seen one. They turn up in small quantities all over the universe, we do not know what they are or where they came from, or even if they are of any use, but they do seem to instil in those who find them a sense of wonder. I did hear of a theory that they were some kind of very ancient communication system, but to and from what, no one knows. They seem to have a life force in them sometimes which we can not understand, but we feel it just the same. Do you intend to take them with us?*'

'Yes, without a doubt. I shan't cut and mount them as I do the other stones, but I feel I must have them.'

'*Fortunately for you, it would seem that you will not have to pay for them.*'

Cresswell thought he almost felt a sense of humour in Vax's remark, and that could only increase the bond between them. It took two journeys to get his hoard of stones and the purple crystals to the exit hatch, and the pile of goods he intended to transfer to the tug was growing out of all proportion to the space available for it.

Refuelling the tug took a lot longer than either of them expected, Vax in the end working out how to do it and completing the task as a bemused Cresswell looked on while his body went through motions he had nothing to do with.

With everything stowed safely on board the tug, he bid farewell to the smelter station, leaving the connecting hatch such that he could enter again should the need ever arise.

The long slow curving sweep out of the smelter's orbit was time consuming, but as the velocity built up the tug was finally on its way out to the asteroid belt and the kind of solitude that Cresswell had always wanted but now knew he had in greater abundance than he actually required.

It was a strange feeling he now experienced, knowing that he was probably the last human being left alive after his fellow human's supreme folly, but he knew he would come to terms with it given enough time.

There was little to do as the tug automatically ploughed its course towards the vast ring of what was thought to have once been a planet, and this gave Cresswell plenty of time to think over the events of the last few, days? Weeks? He wasn't sure just how long it was, so much had happened.

There were several things about Vax which still intrigued him, and there hadn't been the opportunity so far to question him. So it was after he had enjoyed a rare meal of non concentrates which he had managed to salvage from the smelter station's deep freeze, that he got down to some serious questioning.

'You said some time ago that you and your kind have been keeping an eye on us for a while, but you didn't exactly explain why you thought this was necessary, and what there was in it for you.'

'There are many races of peoples out here in the galaxy, most of which are happy to trade goods and information, technology and expertise, but it would upset the general status quo and possibly the stability of all that we have built up over aeons of time, if an unstable race of people like yours were to be let loose among us. It is to this end that we monitor all races which look as if they are going to develop space travel, in order to prevent the unstable ones from leaving their own solar systems. It may seem a harsh thing to do, but it is for the greater good of all that a few must possibly suffer, although they don't usually realize it.'

'I can't argue with that, but how could you stop us once we had developed a drive which would take us out of our system?'

'Accidents happen.'

'Oh, as simple as that. What if the race finds out what you are doing?'

'They never do, not as far as I know. But then we do not have to refuse many, which is perhaps fortunate.'

'What we've just seen happen to Earth, does that happen very often?'

'No, not in proportion to those who develop in the expected way, but it can and does happen, so I am told.'

'Could your people have prevented our holocaust, moved in and stopped it before it got out of hand, told us about the others out there?'

'Yes, we could have, but it would have been against the rules of development set down a very long time ago, and we could never have been sure of the stability factor. We would have broken a very old code of conduct had we interfered with your natural development. It was something you had to work out for yourselves.'

'I can understand your point of view, but it does seem a terribly unnecessary waste of life.'

'Balanced against the amount of life, as you put it, in the known universe, it was only a tiny speck and will not be missed. Consider the consequences if these rules were not held rigorously in place.'

Cresswell did, and had to admit that Vax and his rules were for the best, in the long run.

There were many more discussions as the tug drove on towards the belt, interspersed with a little gem cutting and mounting by Cresswell to give him time to think over some of the things which Vax came up with.

At one point Vax asked if he could take over Cresswell's body and try his hand at working a gem.

He watched in a strangely detached way as his hands moved under their own volition, turning the stone this way and that until Vax had decided just how he would cut the stone. The result, after many hours of painstaking work was a wonder to behold, and Cresswell felt deeply moved in a way he had never experienced before at the sheer beauty and brilliance of the finished product.

'In my world you could make a very good living at this, I've never seen such work, and I very much doubt if anyone else has.'

'Thank you for your acknowledgement of my effort. I have enjoyed it very much, and would if you do not mind, like to cut another stone sometime. This is a new experience for me, something I would never have thought of doing, I thank you for introducing me to this new art form.'

'Good God, it's his first stone, and he turns out something like this! It's not fair.' Cresswell couldn't stop the thought from forming before it was too late, and knowing that Vax would experience it too, tried to stop it, but it was too late.

He wasn't sure if it was real or he imagined it, but there was a feeling of pride emanating from his companion. Cresswell was justly pleased with that.

A soft 'ping' from the auto pilot warned him that they were nearing their destination, and he took up his position at the controls for the final approach to the outer limits of the asteroid belt.

The first few lumps of rock at the edge of the belt twinkled faintly in the weak rays of the far distant sun, reminding him just how far they were from all that was home and familiar, but this was going to be his new home now, there was nowhere else to go.

'I'll take the tug to the point where I first met you and see what has happened to your ship, there may be some bits and pieces you would like to salvage.'

'*I do not think there will be, but do go if you want to.*'

Cresswell checked the co-ordinates he had recorded when he first picked up the distress call, fed them into the auto pilot and sat back in his chair.

'You know, you never did tell me how you managed to occupy my body, and without me knowing about it until much later.'

'It is a long story, but I will tell you if you wish.'

'I wish.'

A very long time ago, I did a great service to a race of people who can do this 'joining' quite naturally, and by way of showing their gratitude, they taught me how to do it. There was a proviso however, and that was it must only be done when there is no alternative and my survival is at stake, and then only with the permission of the person I am to share with, and for the shortest possible time.

I have never actually needed to do it before, and it was only because I was in a desperate situation that I shared with you. I have been out of my body for short periods before, but the thought of being stranded for aeons of time out here in the belt was more than I could accept. I knew fear for the first time, a deep and dreadful fear which I will not recall, as I suspect that you are now able to pick up some of my thoughts, and I would not want you to experience it.'

'But you didn't ask my permission, you said 'can I share with you' and I thought you meant share my tug, so of course I agreed and I took your body back with me, but it died.'

'I am sorry, there was a misunderstanding, I did not make myself clear in what I was asking of you, and that was my fault.'

'I don't think you were in a state to make anything clear to anyone, your body was crushed to a pulp by the collapsing ship, and I still don't know how you managed to stay in it, I couldn't have done, not with that much pain. Anyway, it has worked out well, without you I wouldn't have survived until now, that's for sure, so there are no complaints on my part, in fact I'm very grateful for what you've done'

I am pleased to be of help to you, and I must admit I have enjoyed our shared experiences, they were like nothing I have ever known before.'

'There is one thing I've noticed since we decided to come back to the asteroid belt, and that's you're a lot happier, or pleased, or something like that, I'm not sure what it is exactly. Why?'

'Mainly because there is a remote chance that we might be rescued.'

'By whom or what? There's nothing out here but rock, none of my people will have survived even if their tugs have.

'Remember the reason for my being here in the first place? My replacement will have been sent at the appointed time, and by now his replacement, and possibly another, so there is a chance that contact may be made and a rescue effected.'

'But you could have done that in the beginning rather than going back to Earth, why didn't you?'

'For two reasons. I owed you something I could not repay in full, and you were very keen to return. As long as I could help you to keep your body alive, it did not matter to me if we spent a little time returning to your home planet, and you would not have been happy if we had not done so. The other reason was that I did not know if a replacement had arrived, and there was no means of making contact.'

'We still don't know how to make contact.'

'When we found those purple crystals, I have had a feeling that they may be the link we need. I do not know how it will work, but there is something about them that will help us.'

'If we are rescued, what will happen to us? I suppose you will go back to your home planet, but what about me? Can I live there?'

'Not really, although the atmosphere is very similar, the oxygen content is far too high for your metabolism, and your body would age very quickly. We would have to get you another body.'

'Oh, come on, that's not possible, you can't just go around putting people into different bodies!'

'Why not? I was able to join you in yours, so it can not be too difficult for you to transfer to another one, if you wish to do so. We may need to seek the help of those who gave me the technique to join you, but I think it could be done.'

'All right, I've nothing to lose. But it feels a little scary!'

'I know how you feel.'

'I'll bet you do!'

And they both laughed together.

The conglomeration of rock which had entrapped Vax's ship so long ago was located, but the formation had changed shape, and there was no sign of the alien ship.

'Probably ground to dust by now.'

'More than likely. I would very much doubt if there was anything worth salvaging anyway, the communication unit was the first thing to be destroyed.'

The alien ship masquerading as an asteroid was found without much difficulty, but when they tried to get into the tunnel which led down to the power control room, the doorway wouldn't open for them, try as they might, so they gave up on that idea.

The tug was put into a stable orbit well clear of any wandering asteroids, and the business of locating Vax's replacement began.

'How are we going to do this?' asked Cresswell, unable to comprehend the difficulties of using a different language to his own, and not knowing one word of it.

'I think, as I have said before, the crystals are the link, perhaps we should start with them.'

'OK, but what do we do with them?'

'Choose one, and let us see what happens.'

Cresswell went to the locker where he had put the deep purple crystals, and was surprised to see one of them gently glowing, a soft light radiating from deep within the crystalline matrix.

He removed it gently and with a sense of reverence, almost afraid to touch it lest he should contaminate it with something of his unworthy being.

'God, that's a strange feeling. Are you sure we're doing the right thing?'

'Yes, I think so. I do not sense any danger, but there is the feeling of an awful lot of power here. We must be very careful what we do.'

Cresswell sat down, cradling the crystal in his hands and wondering what to do next, but any decision was taken from him as he felt Vax take over control.

His hands turned the crystal into a vertical position, and then the sensation of being drawn into the purple depths began.

At first, Cresswell's eyes went out of focus and the crystal took on a hazy appearance, growing in size until it seemed to fill the whole cabin, and then out into space to encompass the whole universe.

He and the crystal became one, with Vax somewhere in the background. He could sense him there, doing something, but he didn't know what it was.

The singing sound came a little later, as Cresswell floated in a nothingness, oblivious to all around him except the deep purple haze which seemed to hold and caress him in its wonderful glow.

Somewhere, something responded, the singing tone was joined with another tone which sounded like a harmonic of the first. The intensity of the duet grew until Cresswell's head hurt, messages flashed back and forth across the universe, translated several times, answered and sent back again, and then the singing was gone, and the internal light of the crystal slowly faded as Cresswell's eyes came back into focus.

He was sweating and trembling as he sat in the chair, the crystal now just a beautiful lifeless thing, still held firmly in his wet and shaking hands.

'I'm not to sure I want to go through that again, beautiful and painful and .... something I can't quite put my finger on.'

'It was indeed a strange experience for me too, but it was quite benign. I think we have made ourselves known to someone, somewhere, but I am not too sure who. We will have to wait and see what happens next. I do not think we will be abandoned, somehow.'

Cresswell put the crystal back in the locker with the other two, but he went to see them many times, just to admire the sheer beauty of them and to remind himself of the singing.

The tug cruised among the asteroids, exploring the shattered remains of a once great planet, looking for anything unusual rather than of material value.

Many strange pieces of mineral were found, some recognized as being in a different form than he had encountered before, but there were many more which defied identification.

Vax, using Cresswell's hands, cut some more stones and mounted them in a matrix of sparkling silver filigree which he had somehow spun.

The rations were noticeably going down by the time the object scanner picked up the mass of something large and in a great hurry coming towards them.

The warning blast from the detector snapped him from a light sleep, and he positively hurled himself into the control seat, winding the visual scanner up to full magnification. A tiny dot of light could just be seen on the edge of the scanner plate, growing in size as he watched.

'I hope it has seen us and stops in time, otherwise we'll be knocked into another dimension if it hits us.'

'I think it has begun deceleration already, we have nothing to fear.'

The dot had grown in size to fill half the screen and Cresswell had to cut the magnification down to normal so that he could get some idea of its distance.

A glow of energy flared out from the ship like an all consuming flame, fading as it reached out into the space around the craft, and then the alien ship just stopped, hanging there in space, a mere few hundred metres away from the little tug.

'Are these your people?' asked an anxious Cresswell, wondering what to do if the answer was in the negative.

'Yes, but the ship looks a little different to those which I remember. You had better switch on your communication system to open frequency, they may well try to contact us using radio waves first.'

The quiet hum of the receiver was suddenly disrupted by a burst of sound which set his ears ringing.

'We have contact of a sort, but I can't understand a word of it.'

'Do not worry, let me take over, I will speak to them.'

Cresswell relaxed back in the control seat, suddenly a great weight seemed to lift from his shoulders which he hadn't been aware of before. Someone had found them, and they would be rescued from eternal wanderings among the asteroids, or until his food ran out, which was the more likely event.

As usual when Vax took over, Cresswell seemed to slip into the background, not that he was unaware of what was going on, but it seemed a slight dreamlike haze through which he viewed and listened, but had no physical control.

Vax was making his mouth utter a strange language, not one word of which he could understand, while his ears received the replies and Vax somehow interpreted them.

The conversation went on for some time, back and forth, between Vax and the alien ship, and then contact was broken, Cresswell suddenly regaining full awareness.

'They will come over to the tug and take us across to their ship, leaving the tug here in orbit. We will then be taken back to my world, so that we can set about finding some means of getting you a new body. Although we are humanoid, we are not quite like you, so do not be alarmed when you see us in our true form. Do not forget, you only saw me in my space suit, and I know you thought I was just like you.'

'I don't think anything could scare me after what we've been through, so don't worry on my behalf. In fact, I'm rather keen to meet your people, they at least sound reasonably civilized.'

'It is suggested that you bring a good supply of food and breathing packs so that you do not have to breathe our air. Later, if your air supply runs out, we will make a device which will dilute the oxygen in our air so that you do not suffer premature ageing. Any of your coloured stones and cutting equipment you wish to take along, with anything else of value to you, should be left by the hatchway. They say to wish you well, and long life.'

There was a sharp rap on the hatch door, and when Cresswell opened it two space suited figures beckoned him out, and escorted him across to the waiting alien ship.

The air lock was not too dissimilar to his own, but once inside the ship, things were very different.

He kept pace with his two escorts as they quickly strode up a long corridor and into a large comfortable looking room. It was nothing like he thought a spaceship should be, it was more like the rest room back on the smelter station.

'We will sit down here and wait for the rest of the crew to collect your things, and then we will be introduced, and give our explanation for what has happened.'

They didn't have long to wait. There was a general scurrying about, heard rather than seen, and then the ship was under-way, not that Cresswell realized that.

A tall stately figure came into the room and that was when he got his first shock.

'I know, you think he is like one of the gods you have in your myths,' Vax said to Cresswell. 'He only looks like one! It is customary to be on your feet to greet another, I would suggest that you stand up.'

Cresswell did, and snapped to attention, or did the best he could within the confines of his space suit.

'There is no need to be formal, we have what you would refer to as a chain of command, but there is no formality here, we are all equal, it is *just that we do different jobs with different responsibilities.'*

The figure before him was a good two metres high, jet black close cropped hair adorned a face which looked as if it had been chiselled out of a deep amber coloured granite.

Two almond shaped brilliant blue eyes peered out from a ridged forehead, beneath which was a squat stubby nose with a slit for a mouth. The forward thrusting chin looked as if it would cut stone with no trouble at all, while a thick set neck joined the whole to a body built to strike fear at a Mr. Universe competition.

It wasn't over large or heavy looking, just very solid and well muscled to a degree which would create extreme envy in most human males.

Vax must have told the Captain what humans expected when meeting, for he strode forwards, extending a perfectly manicured hand and grasped Cresswell's, giving it a firm grip and a single shake.

His slit like mouth opened and a stream of unintelligible sounds issued forth, which Vax promptly translated.

'Welcome to our ship. Vax has told me what you have done in sharing your body with him and we are grateful to you for this. It is the wish of Vax that you be given a new body, and although I do not know how this is to be done, we will co-operate in any way we can. We are heading back to Vax's home world where he will organize the transfer. We are sorry to learn of what has happened to your race, but do not feel too badly about it, we think it was inevitable from the start. Your people did not have a chance from the beginning, it was the way things were set up.'

'What does he mean, 'inevitable from the start'? The start of what?'

'I think I should explain that a little later, after you have got fully used to the idea of other races and feel comfortable with the idea. There is a lot more to whom and what we are than you can imagine, but now is not the time to discuss it. I hope that is all right with you?'

'Yes, I suppose so, I don't think I have any option anyway.'

Cresswell was taken around the ship, everything being explained to him in great detail until his senses were overwhelmed. What amazed him most was the apparent simplicity of everything, the technological wizardry being concealed behind simple facades and therefore creating a false impression from his point of view.

They had fitted him up with a small cubicle in which they were able to dilute the normally oxygen rich air of the ship with an extra amount of nitrogen gas, thus saving his body from the ravishing effects of the free radicals which would have otherwise been formed had they not done so.

It also meant that he was able to eat in comfort and attend to his ablutions when necessary, although the suit did cater for that contingency in a rudimentary way.

One of the crew, who was interested in Cresswell's history, had tried to sit with him in his special room, but had to be taken out after a while, his normally amber coloured face going a dirty purple and showing great signs of distress.

Once he had seen most of the ship, he spent quite long periods of time in his special cubicle.

'Although I'm used to being in a suit for long periods, it's nice to get out of the damn thing and move about freely.'

'I can feel a difference in your body movements when you are in here, so I can appreciate how you must feel. It will be much better when we reach my home world, we can make you a special dwelling in which you can have your normal air until the transfer can be arranged.'

'I still don't see how we can be transferred to other bodies. Will we be able to remember this life? I don't like the idea of being someone else with another set of memories which don't belong to me.'

'It is not like that, believe me. I can not explain the exact details to you now, but with the help of the people who gave me the ability to join you, I think we can make the switch.'

'And I will still be me? If you see what I mean?'

'Yes, just as I am still me, as you put it, when I am in with you. We still think as two different people, and there is a difference when I take your body over, but we still remain individuals, each with our own way of thinking, and our own set of memories.'

'God, I hope you're right.' said an unconvinced Cresswell.

The great ship sped on through the galaxy from lay point to lay point, so avoiding the intricate manoeuvres which would be necessary if it had to pass through the more densely populated solar systems scattered in its path.

They had passed two black holes, but were unaffected by the mighty gravitational forces from them due to the velocity the ship had attained, enabling the crew to observe the awesome phenomena without any danger to themselves.

Cresswell was impressed with the apparent nonchalance of those on board to what he considered the ultimate nightmares of the physical universe, but as he had only known of them in theory, his fears were lessened by his lack of actual experience of these cosmic vacuum cleaners.

In his cubical one shift, he was looking at his naked body in the highly reflective end wall, just prior to a wash down and general tidy up of his somewhat unkempt hair, when Vax interrupted his thoughts.

'Why do you think so little of your body? What do you see about it that you despise?'

'It's a puny pale thing compared to the rest of the crew and I would be embarrassed for them to see me like this.'

'But why? It is a fine body, and would be much admired among your fellow men.'

'I doubt that. Anyway, there aren't any left, remember?'

'You sometimes have an attitude which I find hard to understand. You must realize that bodies are designed, or as you think of it, evolved, to meet the circumstances in which they have to survive. A body is only a vehicle, and a vehicle must be made to suit the environment in which it will operate. Yours is well constructed to suit your world, as our bodies are to the different conditions we have to face. Wait until you meet some of the other peoples of the galaxy, you will find much to amuse you then, and will think better of your own.'

He finished his ablutions wondering just what he was going to see, and how he would react to it when he did.

Cresswell began a regime of exercises, partly to pass the time but mainly to increase his musculature, much to the amusement of Vax, for whom vanity had very little meaning and no value whatsoever.

He didn't make a great deal of progress with it however, until Vax showed him how to stress one set of muscles against another, so building them up and expending much less energy in the process.

By the time the great ship began to decelerate within the bounds of its home system, he was looking in fine shape, and apart from his still very pale skin colour, was almost as well built as the rest of the crew.

The ship went into orbit around its home world, and he was advised to gather his scant belongings together for the journey down to the planet's surface.

He would still have to wear his breathing pack until they had constructed a suitable home for him with its own air supply, and it had already been decided that a small extra room should be added to the abode with a transparent thin film divider so that natives of the planet could visit him, and through Vax, hold a conversation without either of them having to suit up.

The planet to ship shuttle came gracefully curving up from below, a bright twinkling star in its own right, and Cresswell admired the skill of the pilot as he swept the craft around to dock in one easy manoeuvre.

Through Vax, he said his goodbyes to the crew, and the Captain in particular, who still towered above him despite all his efforts, although he could almost match him muscle for muscle.

The first sight of Vax's home world was something of a surprise for Cresswell as he had expected to see a vast city spread out before him as the shuttle came in to land. Instead, there was just a modest collection of buildings spread out on each side of the long runway, albeit beautifully designed to blend in with the rolling countryside, the building's colours adding to the general ambience of peace and tranquillity.

The shuttle glided in with hardly a sound, touching down gently on the pale grey landing strip and then slowing down to stop opposite one of the larger buildings.

'This isn't your main space port, is it?' he asked, still surprised at the modesty of the place.

'No, it is just one of several shuttle landing places we have, the two main trading ports are much bigger and busier. We try to keep most of our transport systems disguised or underground, as it would be a shame to spoil the countryside, but landing from space necessitates an open air approach. I think it blends in well.'

A ramp was brought up to the exit hatch, and he was gently led out by two of the crew to greet a small crowd who had gathered beside the runway.

He raised his hand in salute, and the crowd hesitatingly responded by doing likewise in what they thought was the correct response, never having seen one of his kind before.

The reception party surprised Cresswell, although he didn't know for sure if it was for him or the returning Vax. It didn't matter really, they all had a good time, although the space suit restricted his full enjoyment to some degree.

A few days later and he had his new home, built from prefabricated units and assembled after much discussion with him as to how he would like it constructed.

Nothing seemed too much trouble for these people, and Cresswell began to wonder why they were making such a fuss to get everything just to his liking.

The concentrates were brought in, a water supply laid on, and he began to feel at home, or at least as much at home as he could on an alien world and being the only one of his kind. He wondered how he would have faired if it hadn't been for the company of Vax, but didn't dwell on it too long as the thought made him feel definitely uneasy.

It wasn't long before some of the concentrates had been analysed by his hosts, and a more acceptable form of food supplied. He was a little concerned at first that it might not agree with his digestive system, but was assured, through Vax, that it matched exactly the main ingredients of the concentrates and would prove quite harmless, and certainly tastier.

Cresswell had barely settled in when he received the first of many requests for an interview by one of the locals who was interested in the history of his home world.

At first he couldn't see why anyone this far away from earth should have an interest in his planet or him, except as a curiosity maybe. It turned out that a small team of researchers were compiling a history of every planet their explorations had ever discovered, and how their races developed.

In a way, Cresswell felt ashamed of his people and what they had brought upon themselves, and was reluctant to divulge much in the way of real data until Vax gave him a good talking to.

'I do not understand your attitude about relating your people's history. You seem to think that you are one and the same as them. This is not so, you are a separate entity with your own set of values and morals. You did not subscribe to their way of life, and when you found there was nothing you could do about it, you did the only thing possible so as not to compromise yourself, you left their company. You had no choice in being placed among them, so why do you think you are of them?'

'Put like that, it's hard to argue back, but I still don't like it very much.'

'That is fair comment. You do not have to talk to them if you do not wish to, no one will force you to do so. They are just a team of people who wish to compile all the data they can on how races develop, so that one day maybe, they can assist others who need a little help.'

'But I thought you said you weren't allowed to interfere with a developing race.'

'That is so, but if a race asks for help, then it may be given in a very tightly controlled manner, but they have to reach for that help, it is not given without considerable thought first.'

'All right, you've made your point, I'm being churlish again I suppose. I'll do my best to co-operate.'

The following day Cresswell apologized to the two historians who were so keen to learn of his people and their demise, and a much more friendly relationship developed, Cresswell suggesting that they begin again with their enquires.

He still felt a little uneasy due to the fact that they didn't look as friendly as they actually were, due mainly to the difference in physical appearance, their very set and stern faces belying their true nature.

'Can you tell us when your people first displayed an aggressive attitude towards their fellows?'

'As far as I know, and I can only go by the history of my people that was available to me when I was a young man and learning about such things, it must have been when they first developed. According to history, small groups of men and women would live together in what we call a clan, and would defend that group against others who would try to take from them their women folk or anything else they chose, like food or animal stock. They were very primitive, living in caves or grass huts with very little in the way of tools as we know them.

As time went by, trading took the place of these raids. As a basic illustration, those living near the sea would exchange fish with those who lived in the nearby forests for fruit and nuts.

Eventually this got a bit complicated, and tokens, which we call credits, were used in place of direct exchanges. I would value my produce as being worth ten credits, and would receive a token representing that value, which I could then exchange for the goods I required to the same value, or if it was worth more than ten credits, I would have to give more.

This system, in the beginning, stopped many groups from just taking what they wanted from others, but then something else happened, which has led to the present disaster on earth.

There were many different races on earth. At one time they were in groups dotted about the planet, and kept much to themselves, but as time went by, they spread out and mixed with each other, going into each others areas, but instead of truly mixing, they tended to stay in their own groups within those other areas.

It was the difference in ideals, beliefs and physical looks which really caused the main troubles. They became intolerant of each other, and this seemed to reinforce their own beliefs to a point of fanaticism where ideals became out of all proportion to the facts. There were many wars between these different peoples, but in time, as weapons became more sophisticated and reached the capability of mass destruction on a grand scale, a sort of uneasy peace developed, as each nation realized that total war would result in total destruction, and no one would win.

By this time, the small nations had combined to form three main nation states, almost of equal size and ability. The warring then took on the form of trading and financial aggression, each trying to out do the other and weaken them in any way possible.

What actually precipitated the final conflict, I don't know, as I wasn't on earth at the time. All I do know is that upon returning to what was once a beautiful planet, there were no humans left that I could find, only machines who were still carrying on the pointless war. The earth, when I left it was in total ruins, all the cities destroyed and very little left to show where man had once been.'

'We feel sad that such a thing should have befallen your people. Vax has informed us that you feel a loneliness which we can only imagine, but have little reality on. You are not alone here, we are of like kind to you, although we may have physical differences.

There is one point we would like to explore a little further. You mentioned that there were many different races on your world from the beginning of your recorded history. This phenomenon has been encountered before, and in every case, has resulted in the same outcome, destruction on a grand scale and sometimes total annihilation. We do not understand how so many different races can evolve on one world from the beginning.

We can find no reason why this should be so, as most worlds we have data on only sport one main race, with very little differences between isolated groups. Eventually they progress to become members of the great collection of worlds which Vax has told you about. What we are trying to resolve is the fact that many different worlds with a great diversity of peoples can get on with each other, but different races on one planet can not.'

'I have no answer to that, I only wish I did. There must be some common factor which causes these people to be so aggressive.'

Cresswell shrugged his shoulders, feeling he should say more, but not knowing what. The pause between them lengthened almost to the point of embarrassment, and then he remembered something.

'There is one thing which may be a clue, although I don't see how it fits in at the moment. We are taught that we came, or evolved, from a type of animal. I don't see that somehow, and never did. It just doesn't ring true, there are far too many lose ends with the theory.

Anyway, we are supposed to have evolved from a simple humanoid type of creature who ate fruit and spent most of the day scratching itself, to the present human form with a high degree of intelligence, although the intelligent bit is up for questioning after what's happened. There is one thing wrong about that, there is a big time gap between the humanoid state and the appearance of the different races around the planet. They appeared, overnight, with regard to the time scale involved, and that leaves just too many unanswered questions for my liking.

Where did they come from? They couldn't have evolved because there's no record of that happening, and they all appeared in a relatively short period of time. As groups they seemed to stay in their own areas for a considerable length of time, and then moved out to interface with other groups, and that was when the real troubles began.'

'There is one thing we have found which may have a bearing on the situation, and that is most planets of this nature do seem to have one race of people which does seem to have evolved from their own animal stock, but the others do not, and we can not find out how they came about. It would seem that at the time of introduction, history was not recorded in such a manner as to be accessible to us for evaluation, nor are there any traces of events leading up to the introduction of the different species within the race.'

Cresswell was beginning to get really interested in the discussion when he had to call a halt to the proceedings as his voice was getting rough. Vax had to use his vocal cords for translation purposes with regard to the pair of researchers, and his larynx wasn't used to some of the sounds which Vax made. A break was called, and they agreed to meet again next day.

'Glad you gave me that metaphorical kick in the backside, it's what I needed to shake me out of the state of non confront I've been in ever since we went down to earth.'

'I felt I had to, as you could have missed so much interesting data and maybe the chance to resolve the reasons for your race's demise.'

There were more meetings over the next few days, and although ideas were batted back and forth, they were no nearer to solving the problem of why things sometimes go so wrong on some worlds.

Cresswell was very pleased to be free of the confines of his space suit within his new home, but he still had to wear it when he went out to view the world of Vax and his people.

The visits were organized quite frequently by a local group of people who had concerned themselves with the situation he and Vax had found themselves in.

All the people Vax had known were long gone, and to him it was like making new friends again in an almost strange world, as so much had changed in the time he had been away. They were able to share the new discoveries together, which increased the natural bond between them, each learning a little of how the other saw things from a different point of view.

A visit to one of the underground factories which supplied the local community with just about all their needs caused much raising of his eyebrows.

'Here you see just what machines are capable of when properly applied to the needs of those they serve, and I am not making a point about this, just a statement of fact.'

'Oh, come on Vax, that one was just too good to miss up! I'd have undoubtedly got that one in if the boot had been on the other foot.'

There was silence for a moment, and then the laugh echoed between them, causing several of the accompanying staff to give questioning looks as they were not in on the joke, but could see its effects on Cresswell's body.

'I can see where the manufactured goods come from, but what about the fruit, vegetables and grain you must need?'

They are grown in large areas well shielded from general view, but of course can be visited if anyone wishes to. You might think that the landscape is natural, but it is not so.

We have taken what nature has provided and added to it, being very careful to blend everything in so that it looks natural. I am told there is a valley near here which is worth a visit, we will go to it when we return to the surface.'

The tour of the underground factory more than impressed him, it left him speechless. It was so quiet and clean, the machines softly murmuring away to each other while products sped along moving slide ways to disappear into holes in the wall and on to their destinations.

'There are very few things which are not made by machines, the main exceptions being those things which people want to make by hand for the sheer joy of doing so.

I well remember building a time keeping mechanism, it took a great deal of time to make all the parts, and even longer to get them to work such that the time was kept fairly accurately, but it still was not as good as one of the ordinary crystal controlled timekeepers everyone has about their person for everyday use. But I did get a great deal of enjoyment out of the exercise'

After leaving the factory, and still in the company of their guides, the little troupe set off for the valley Vax had been told about. The journey took them through one of the large fruit growing areas and Cresswell watched fascinated as machines glided along the rows of trees seeking out ripe fruit, gently taking it from the trees and placing it in carriers ready for distribution.

'Everything seems so calm and well organized, so what is there for the people to do?'

'Plenty. They do whatever they want to. The two historians are fully occupied, there are a few people in the underground factory who enjoy looking after the machines down there, you will find that everyone does whatever they think needs to be done, consummate with their skills. It is structured a little differently to the life you have been used to, as we are all different in our requirements.'

'It's a great pity we didn't have something like this on earth, perhaps things wouldn't have turned out so badly then.'

'It would have made little difference to the outcome, it is the people, not the system, which dictates how things will develop.'

The mobile rounded a bend in the track and before them was one of the highest waterfalls Cresswell had ever seen.

It began almost up among the clouds where the mountain brushed against the sky, a thin thread of white water tracing its way down over a series of rocky ledges to fall several hundred metres onto a large scoop shaped stone where it was joined by another stream coming in from the side. A series of rocky slabs jutted out from the main cliff face and wound down in a spiral pattern, the water cascading from one to the next in a glittering shower of silver droplets to eventually pour over yet another stone lip, splitting into two streams as it did so, and that was only one tenth of the drop.

The sheer height of the fall made him feel a little dizzy and Vax picked up his feelings.

'I am always surprised when things like this affect your sense of balance, and yet you quite happily don your space suit and wander out among the stars!'

'It's not quite the same thing, but I do see what you mean. I don't quite understand it either.'

Cresswell felt he could watch the passage of the water falling through its winding path to the valley below all day, there was so much detail to take in.

Through Vax, one of the guides explained the history of the waterfall.

A long time ago there were several falls with many little streams feeding them from the side of the mountain. Someone made a picture of the falls as you see them now, and it was agreed that it would look more beautiful and harmonious with the surrounding scenery if the many streams were made into one. It took a long time and an awful lot of work, but the result is well worth it.'

'You must have moved mountains of rock to do this, and yet it looks quite natural, as if nature had set it up like this.'

'You see,' said Vax, *'There is plenty to do if you want to be occupied.'*

They stood there for some considerable time, drinking in the majesty of the scene, their eyes tracing the ever changing path of the water as it made its way down through the cascades to the valley below.

Many more trips into the hinterland of the centre where Cresswell had his new home brought new discoveries and many thought provoking items of interest, not least of which was the synthetic protein generation plant.

Strictly speaking, it wasn't synthetic, nor was it a generator in the true sense of the word.

Perhaps the definition of the process had lost a little in the translation from the native tongue to Cresswell's somewhat cumbersome language.

They had found a way of growing animal tissue in vast tanks of nutrient, so that they could use it for food without actually having to kill animals. For him, it was difficult to comprehend the finer points of the process, but basically a small amount of tissue from a chosen organ was painlessly extracted and then grown on in vitro, and later genetically modified so that it was interdependent of the need for surrounding tissues which would be required in the normal state.

This produced huge pieces of meat fibre which could then be removed from the vats and processed as normal animal meat would have been. The real beauty of the process was that the fat, fibre and collagen content of the product could be accurately controlled to produce a highly concentrated food protein with none of the unpleasantness of using actual animals, which had long been abhorrent to Vax's people.

The automated factories fascinated him to the degree that he returned many times to watch the machines flawlessly producing very complex goods without the need for human intervention at any point in their manufacture.

'How did all this mechanical production begin?' he asked one day.'

'As on your world, electronics developed to the point where their abilities far outstretched the current applications, and people began looking for things for the new advanced processors to do. In the beginning, it was 'put a processor into everything', but then people began looking for things the new science could do which would lessen the more mundane side of work. As sensors became ever more sophisticated, it was relatively easy to automate most work processes, and that had led up to what you see today. A similar thing must have happened on your world, but the wrong path was taken at an early stage, resulting in what we sadly observed.'

Cresswell still found it difficult to accept the fact that machines had almost acquired the same faculties as humans with regard to their ability to judge and correct their actions.

These machines were more sophisticated and advanced than anything he had seen on earth.

It was just after a long session with the 'history investigators' that Cresswell was visited by a member of the science faculty, smartly turned out in a deep midnight blue uniform complete with silver epaulettes.

'We have managed to contact the people who taught Vax the sharing method, and have explained the fact that there are two of you in the same body, and that you both would like to be assigned new bodies.

At first they wanted nothing to do with the idea, but relented when we explained that Vax was one of those entrapped. They will send someone to see if anything can be done about it, and we will tell you as soon as we have any more information on the subject.'

Now that there was chance of freedom from the encumbrance of the space suit every time he wanted to go outside his home, he had doubts about the actual transfer to a new body. Although Vax had joined him in his, he didn't like the idea of transfer himself. Would he remember who he was? Would it be an adult body, and which sex? Or would it be like starting all over again as a baby?

Vax wasn't much help when questioned on the subject, as he hadn't experienced that kind of transfer either, so they were both left in the dark as to exactly what would happen, if it did happen, and that wasn't a certainty.

The longer he and Vax shared the same body, the more they began to think of themselves as one unit rather than two separate beings. Vax was the first to notice this, and brought the subject up one day as

Cresswell was lazing in the sun just outside the house.

Cresswell, fed up with the restrictions imposed by the space suit, had abandoned its use for short periods while he lay out in the warm glow of the early morning sun, trying to reduce the possible damage to his body by controlling his breathing to a low and shallow rate. His argument was that if they were to get new bodies, then it didn't matter too much if he let his present one age a little due to the excess oxygen, and if the transfer didn't work, then what the hell, he'd become an old wrinkly a little before his appointed time.

Vax saw the possible long term effects of this, and although he didn't discourage Cresswell, he wasn't too happy about it, and that was what he picked up without Vax having to verbalize his thoughts.

'You know, we are beginning to think as one these days, I am picking up your pictures of things you think about complete with all the emotions that go with them. Do you think we are becoming a single unit, melding into one being?'

'I do not see how this could happen, but I do understand how you could think it so. For a long time I have experienced this phenomenon, this was why I was able to anticipate your actions and step in to correct them if necessary. I am pleased that you feel this way, as it indicates that the barriers between us are fading away, and a higher degree of trust now exists.'

'I'm not too sure about this transfer thing now, suppose it goes wrong and they can't split us apart or get us into new bodies? What happens to us? Where do we go, or do we just cease to exist?'

'Unfortunately, I have no data on that, it has never happened to me before, an actual transfer that is. It was easy joining you, I had no alternative if I wished to survive as a being. I just instinctively used the skills taught me by that race I told you about. I didn't even have to think about it once you agreed, although you did not fully understand what was involved.'

'I must say I have no regrets about what happened, it has been a very enlightening experience for me, and if the circumstances came up again I would go along with it. No doubt about that.'

'For that I thank you, I too have enjoyed our joining, if that is the right word. I owe you a debt which I feel I shall have a great deal of trouble paying back.'

'There's nothing to pay back, you have helped me to survive, in fact I wouldn't have made it without your constant watchfulness and intervention in moments of crisis, so the score is as even as it ever can be.'

The bond between them had grown to such an extent that it was to have an effect later on when they were separated, and gave rise to much research on behalf of the scientific community.

It was some time later when the envoy from the planet which was to effect the transfer arrived, and by then Cresswell had got used to the idea of his new life, and was in a way reluctant to go ahead with the separation.

It wasn't just the underlying fear that something might go wrong with the process, but the fact that he had got used to the space suit for external foraging about the planet, and had constructed a simple breathing gadget which diluted the oxygen he breathed when out in the open.

In reality, it was Vax who really wanted to get a new body, and Cresswell could sense his yearning for the event to take place.

The first meeting with the envoy gave Cresswell a jolt he would never forget, and he was surprised that Vax hadn't warned him in advance.

The visit had been arranged for the early afternoon, and he had spruced himself up for the occasion much to the amusement of Vax, who insisted it was completely unnecessary.

Two of the scientific team came in first, turned and took up their positions each side of the doorway.

And then the stranger came in. He was tall, at least two and a half metres of sheer beauty, and he couldn't help but gasp. A cascade of silver white hair framed a golden face, flowing on to almost blend with the scintillating white garment which continued on down to his feet.

The face was one of total calm and serenity, detached from the more mundane things of life, but very much alive.

'*I know, you think it is one of the angels of your old legends.*' Vax murmured.

Cresswell was too overwhelmed to comment back, he just stood there, transfixed to the spot as if time had stood still.

The beautiful one glided across the distance between them until he was within arm's length of the still paralysed Cresswell, extended a hand, palm uppermost, and smiled his angel smile.

He felt his own arm stretch out, palm downwards, and their hands touched, a slight tingling sensation travelling up his arm and out across his whole body.

'*Greetings. I have been advised of the dilemma you both find yourselves in and I understand that it is your joint wish that you be separated and transferred to new bodies.'* The angel smiled again.

'Yes,' said Cresswell, having difficulty forcing the words out. 'I would like to lead a normal life again, without the need for a space suit every time I go outside the confines this building, but I don't want to lose contact with my friend Vax, we have been through a lot together.'

'So I am given to understand. This has not been done with your species or that of your friend before, so there is no certainty that it will be successful, but the chances are in your favour. Do you still wish to go ahead with the transfer?'

'Yes please, we both do.' Cresswell knew he was speaking more for Vax than himself.

'I sense a slight reluctance or hesitation on the part of one of you, it will need total co-operation on both your parts to be successful, perhaps you would like to think it over again. Once the process has begun, it must continue, there can be no going back to your present state as your joint body will slowly cease to function, and will be of no further use to you.'

'I have a feeling it will be all right, I am totally willing to go through with it.' from Vax.

Something seemed to lift from Cresswell, and he suddenly felt more relaxed and at ease with the new body concept.

'Yes, please go ahead, we have nothing to lose really, and everything to gain.'

The angel smiled, but it was a serious smile, and for a moment he felt a twinge of fear, and then it was gone.

'I will give instructions as to what has to be prepared for the transfer. A suitable pair of donors must be found and then your body will be slowly cooled down to a point where you will exteriorise from it and the transfer will be effected. I do not know if you will be aware of this as it is happening, but you must not struggle against it. I will return when I am advised that all is ready.' The golden hand was offered once more, and then the figure turned and wafted from the room in one smooth graceful movement.

Six:
Transformations

THE NEXT DAY the engineers moved into Cresswell's home, taking over one of the rooms and bringing in their equipment.

A long coffin-like box was the first to arrive along with a series of complicated pieces of machinery, the use of which was well beyond his comprehension.

It was while this was being assembled that he requested that they go once more to the waterfall, as it had had such a calming effect on them at their last visit.

They spent the best part of the afternoon watching the thin silver streak of water at the top of the falls gradually grow into the thundering cascade of tumbling foam as it wound its way down to the pool at the bottom of the valley, and then meander its way serenely across the flatlands, weaving in between the various islands and rocky outcrops which dotted its path to the horizon.

It took two days for everything to be set up to the exacting specification laid down by the silver haired one, and he returned on the third day to begin the process of transfer.

Cresswell was led into the room and requested to remove his clothes, and although feeling a little self conscious, did as he was bid.

The tank in the middle of the room had been filled with a liquid which he thought was water, but he didn't like to ask just in case it was something a little more obnoxious and so re stimulate his earlier fears.

Several sticky pads with wires attached were placed about his person, and a thin needle slid painlessly into his upper arm, to be joined up later with a tube which led to one of the many machines around the tank.

They lifted him up and gently lowered his pale body into the fluid which was pleasantly warm, and he began to relax.

Somewhere in the distant background the rhythmic purring of a pump started up, and the temperature of the fluid in the tank began to fall very slightly. He was aware of the change, but it wasn't enough to be uncomfortable yet, and he hoped it wouldn't be.

Was it something in the fluid or was he now resigned to the inevitable? Strangely, he didn't care any more. He just floated there, still in contact with Vax, who uttered frequent calming comments as the temperature of the fluid began to fall even further.

A transparent membrane was lowered over the tank, and it ballooned out to form a curved structure as his special low oxygen air was blown in, and then the surface rippled as the outer door was opened to admit the normal air of the planet so that the attending technicians could breathe without the restrictions imposed by wearing masks.

The angel came up to the head of the tank and placed a golden hand on each side of it, bending down to smile on the now calm features of Cresswell, who then tried to smile back, but found his facial muscles didn't work any more.

It was now decidedly colder, and he could feel a slight tingle in his extremities as the heat was being slowly sucked from his prone body.

He tried to wriggle his toes, but they weren't there any more, or at least he couldn't feel them. Was he dissolving in the fluid? His fingers didn't respond either, and a small flash of panic rippled through him to be dispelled by Vax's calming voice once more.

A sudden flurry of activity around one of the machines took his attention for a moment, the sound of another pump was added to the general background sounds, and then all was calm once more.

Tiny needle like ice crystals began to form around the sides of the tank and slowly crept towards the prone figure of Cresswell, adorning his extremities in a sparkling white crystalline sheath.

'Do you remember when I made the first mounted stone on board the tug?'

'Yes, and I was surprised that we should both think it was so beautiful, despite the differences between us and our cultures. Do you think beauty is a universal thing, recognized by all?'

'No, I do not think so, but we have a lot more in common, despite what you might think, and that is probably why we both like the same things, in general that is.'

The pictures of the mounted stone were as clear as yesterday to him, and he chuckled inwardly as he again watched his fingers under their own volition fashion the stone into something he couldn't have envisaged.

Vax kept Cresswell's attention off the cooling down process by running through the many happy moments they had shared together, steering well clear of the moments of extreme drama which had occurred on the planet during the mechanical's war, lest his heart rate should go up beyond what the technicians required.

The ice crystals insidiously crept closer to the main trunk of Cresswell's body, and as the temperature fell even lower another machine started up, adding a thinning agent to the now turgid blood which was still struggling to course around his chilled blood vessels. He was aware of the coldness, but it didn't hurt so much now, it was more like a soft numbness.

Gradually the room faded from Cresswell's awareness, the sounds of the technicians were now very distant, a mere gentle murmur only just on the edge of his hearing range.

His vision of the transparent dome above his head had long gone, as had the ceiling above that. Only a faint awareness of the room remained, and that was fading fast.

At last the cold didn't hurt any more at all, in fact nothing did, he couldn't feel anything except the sensation of floating, and that began to fade also to be replaced with a sense of nothingness.

He was just he, whoever he was. There was just a space with him in it, neither hot or cold, firm or soft, light or dark.

It was an empty nothingness which he filled to capacity, almost touching the edges, but then there were no edges.

Somehow he could just about sense Vax somewhere, reaching out to him, giving reassurance and comfort, telling him it was all right, and then he also was gone.

✳✳✳

Nature, for want of a better word, had received the biggest setback yet since life had first appeared on planet earth, and was hanging on by its metaphorical finger nails.

Quite apart from the enormous amount of radiation which was released when the nuclear arsenals held by the three main power blocks were randomly discharged at all and sundry, there was one other factor which had nearly brought life on earth to a standstill.

A large nuclear submarine equipped with twenty fission warheads had gone missing off the Marianas Trench near the Philippines, and had settled on a ledge some twelve thousand metres below the surface. The colossal pressure imposed on the hull at this depth eventually caused it to collapse, the resulting implosion being sufficient to cause the nuclear power plant on board to go critical as its controls were disabled.

The force of the explosion plus the intense radiation was just sufficient to trigger the stock pile of nuclear warheads, the resulting concussion wave being all that was needed to release the tension which had built up over several millennia in the two ocean plates far below.

Several kilometres of sea floor moved apart in a horrendous grinding action as the tension was released, exposing the white hot molten magma beneath to the tremendous pressure of the sea water above.

A large portion of the Pacific Ocean promptly fell into this raging furnace of molten rock and was immediately turned into super heated steam, which then blasted its way upwards through the water and straight up into the upper atmosphere, taking sand, silt and the finer particles of the shattered sea floor with it.

This would have been bad enough, but a strange quirk of chance the size of the split plus the immense pressure of the water above it coupled with the temperature differential between the water and the molten magma, caused a pulsing reaction to occur.

As the water rushed in and was turned into super heated steam, it blew the water above it upwards and outwards, causing a huge tidal wave to spread out from its epicentre.

Unfortunately for the land masses around the Pacific Rim, another factor was involved which led to the widespread devastation which was about to occur.

The width of the ocean floor split and the height of the water above it was just right to create a resonant reaction.

When the vast steam column raced upwards and then collapsed, the ocean rushed in again to hit the newly exposed magma which had surged up from the bottom of the trench, causing yet another blast of steam and detritus to heave itself skywards.

The pulsing action just happened to be a harmonic of the tidal wave formation, so each successive wave was now bigger than its predecessor.

As the waves raced towards the shores of the surrounding land masses, the depth of the ocean grew shallower as the sea floor rose to meet that of the land, and the waves rose in height and velocity in consequence.

Each successive wave drove further inland, stripping all before it and turning it into a general soup of vegetation and soil, intermixed with the feeble artefacts of man.

The shock wave from the rent in the ocean floor raced through the rock strata, echoing back and forth and causing the frozen caps of many dormant volcanoes to weaken and break up. The pent-up pressure below the mantle now had a chance to relieve itself, and did so in a most spectacular fashion, spewing forth huge quantities of noxious gasses, ash and aerosols high into the upper atmosphere, where they would cruise around for decades to come before they returned once more to poison the earth.

The pyroplastic flows which coursed down the sides of the volcanoes would normally have settled on the surface of earth, but were now being swept up by the hurricane force winds and carried aloft to circulate for many years to come, occluding the sunlight necessary for life to continue.

The ash and general dust, mixed with the vast amounts of water vapour released from the ocean floor split, turned the clouds a dirty grey colour as they writhed and twisted for space in a limited atmosphere. The only space available was up into the stratosphere, and that is where they went, lightning seething between them as the thunder heads flattened out almost on the borders of space itself.

What the ground shattering waves and the torrential rains, which were to come later, didn't destroy, the radiation, melting polar caps and general darkness brought about by the blocking out of sunlight, did.

The nuclear weapons used were many and varied in their construction, and gave differing levels of fallout, all of which were lethal to just about any life form. Some contained high levels of cobalt which saturated anything they touched with their ferocious gene twisting abilities, and this was later to bring about a series of hideous mutated forms only able to survive by constantly changing into even more grotesque parodies of what was once thought of as normal.

Most of the polar ice caps melted or slipped off their rocky perches, and brought the sea levels up to a point where many low lying lands disappeared altogether, and the old coast lines would have been unrecognisable, if there had been anyone left to observe them.

It wasn't just the extra depth of the oceans due to the melting ice which caused the greatest change, but the fact that once the ice had begun to break up, the ocean currents around the poles sought different routes, or were deflected into different patterns, causing major weather changes just about everywhere.

Before they were inundated by the torrential rains, most of the worlds forests were reduced to ashes by the raging fires caused by the incessant bombardment of one side against the other, and this, coupled with the massive discharge from the volcanoes, raised the carbon dioxide level to a point where the heat from the sun was being trapped and added to by the discharges from the molten magma as it streamed forth from various rents in the earth's surface.

The temperature rose, the air held more water vapour, which in turn held more dust and soon there was very little sunlight reaching the surface of the earth.

Green plants withered and died, and what few animals which had survived, did likewise as their food supplies dwindled.

The vast amounts of water rushing back from the land due to the invasion of the reoccurring tidal waves, washed huge quantities of soil and the remains of man's efforts into the sea, polluting the inshore areas where most of the fish stocks lived, and they perished too.

Once the cloud cover was complete, the rains began, and washed out to sea anything which the returning tides had missed. Vast rivers ripped and tore at the land where little streams had once meandered, gouging out great valleys as they raced towards the lowest point, the ocean.

As the clouds gave up their water, they also gave up their heat, and the temperature began to fall to a more acceptable level, except that there was little left to appreciate the fact.

The vast amounts of dust, ash and acid forming gases which had spewed forth from the volcanoes was eventually washed out of the atmosphere, and the sun occasionally broke through to bathe the barren and riven land with a little soft light.

The very finest of the dusts were the last to succumb to the washing action of the rains, and they tended to collect in pools wherever there was a depression to entrap them, and there they stayed, rich in nutrients, just waiting for something to absorb them and grow.

The slime moulds were the first to take advantage of this free feast, covering the pools with their many coloured wrinkled skins, sprouting spore pods which dusted the local area with more of their kind, but the radiation had done its work and they were like nothing earth had ever seen before.

The next major thrust forward in nature's fight to repopulate earth with living tissue were the fungi.

Where the organic matter from the pulverized forests hadn't been washed out to sea, it had collected in hollows and decomposed. Fine thread-like tendrils of a new breed of fungi appeared, their fruiting bodies rearing up to several metres in height so that their spores could take advantage of the gales, spreading their kind yet further across the wind-swept plains.

Some produced great jelly-like blobs, two or three metres in diameter and in a range of colours which would have made any artist envious, but they relied on being eaten by something to spread their spores, and as there was nothing around which fancied them, they soon died out.

Life, of a sort, was returning to earth's shattered surface.

The first grasses to appear were a little different too, no herbivore would have been able to crop them, let alone digest the tough dark green ribbon-like foliage.

Because of the mutational changes, extra silicon was incorporated in their structure, and this was cross linked on a molecular level to the normal carbon arrangement of the cells, giving them a hitherto unparalleled toughness.

For a time, the new grasses were to be the main covering of the land masses, varying in size and colour to a degree never imagined. Some were only a few millimetres in height, forming a tough green carpet which roamed over everything in sight, their rhizome roots poking into every crevice which contained a little nutrient, and then sending up shoots to cover the new territory in a sward of dark green fibres.

The tallest of the new mutant grasses reached a respectable three to four metres, with brightly coloured seed heads which exploded in the heat of the extra sunlight which was now reaching the surface of the planet, scattering their progeny vast distances to colonize those areas which had remained barren.

It was a long time before the first trees appeared, and they would hardly have been recognized as such, had there been anyone around to do so.

A tall thin whip like stem grew up to several metres in height, with a small crown of sickly yellow green leaves at the top to soak up the available sunlight. The all too frequent gales caused these slender stems to bend and twist, the effected cells in the stem then producing extra fibres to reinforce the stem against further bending motions. This brought about a thickening of the stem which, once begun, would continue so that it looked more like a normal tree trunk, but that was where the similarity ended.

As the tree had absorbed most of the cache of nutrients around its roots, it would then send out a series of side rootlets to a distance equal to its height or until they found another source of food, and these would then send up new stems to form a circular enclosure to the main trunk.

When the new growths had attained approximately the same height as the parent tree in the centre of the group, side shoots from the centre stem would grow out at roughly one or two metre intervals until they touched the new peripheral stems, and when contact was made these side branches would join or meld with the outer stems forming a lateral network bracing the whole plant system against further effects of the gales.

Once the network of branches were firmly joined together, the main centre stem plus the outer ones then grew on up again, repeating the whole process again and again until all nutrients in the area had been used up.

What enabled the trees to continue their spread after their local food stocks had been used up was the fact that some of the stems in the middle of the now not inconsiderable mass of growth, died, and were reabsorbed, so providing further nutrients for those remaining, and as they were now all joined up together, nutrients from far and wide could be pumped along the branches to wherever it was needed.

The polar ice caps began to reform very slowly, removing huge amounts of water from the weather systems and lessening the severity of the storms which still raged around the planet. As the cloud cover returned to a more normal level, the extra sunlight brought forth a burgeoning variety of life forms in the seas and on land, the insects being the first on land in their many mutated forms, filling every niche available.

Creatures with legs and other strange methods of locomotion followed on much later, some small, some gigantic, but all interdependent on each other, mainly as a food source.

The new trees had now grown into massive forests, towering over everything else and forming a home for the ever changing range of creatures brought about by the still present pockets of radiation, which were to persist for a long time to come, causing many more mutations.

In the deeper oceans, many of the old creatures of earth's seas had survived, but the shallower waters of the continental shelves had received massive doses of radiation from direct blasts and radioactive run off from the land masses.

This brought about a new range of sea creatures, plant, animal and fish, the most notable being the giant kelps and bladderwracks. These had colonized the coastal waters for a distance of several kilometres out from the shore line, except where the waters dropped off into the depths and where no sunlight could reach. When all available space in the sea had been taken, they advanced up the beaches, fighting for space to grow and carrying their saline environment with them in long tough conduit-like tendrils.

Once this new method of invasion had been perfected, the distance inland to which they could penetrate was only limited by the ability to transport their salt based life sustaining fluids to the growing tips, and that was quite considerable.

In time, some of them mutated into new forms where they didn't need the salty content of the sea to survive, they made their own from the minerals picked up from the ground, and now they were free to go anywhere, and they did.

Some mutated into creeper-like plants and colonized the new forests, festooning the now massive branches in dark green and brown curtains and shutting out the sunlight from the ground. This brought about a new range of plants which could survive in the almost dark and wet conditions of the forest floor, and a selection of new creeping things which in turn fed upon them.

Change, adapt and survive was the name of the game, and that was happening on a vast scale all over the planet.

It was a long time before the first of the true flying creatures developed. They had come from a series of smaller animals which had grown webs of skin between their legs, enabling them to glide from branch to branch in search of food. Wings eventually developed from a budding at the main joint of the forearm and were covered in a thin skin like membrane.

As is always the case, those who didn't grow a large enough wing span died out as they couldn't hunt proficiently, while this left the more fortunate larger winged varieties to breed on, the wings increasing in area until optimum efficiency had been attained.

There were the occasional bright streaks of light in the night sky as bits of the old smelting stations broke up and their orbits decayed, allowing that which had come from earth to return to its place of origin, until the space around earth was free from all the works of man, only the moon remaining to accompany her as she rotated endlessly around the sun.

By the time the forests had covered most of the suitable land, they had reached a height of several hundred metres, their interlocking branches giving the necessary support to have attained this height against the storm winds.

Life separated out into reasonably stable layers within the vast network of branches, the flying creatures mainly in the lush tree top canopy, while others crept, crawled or jumped at the chosen level which most suited their needs.

The forest floor was almost as dark as night, and here giant albino worms foraged for anything which had been unfortunate enough to have lost its footing or died of old age, and fallen into this twilight world of dampness and decay.

They too, had to move with a fair degree of caution, for waiting for the unwary and hidden within deep holes in the forest floor, there were things very large and perpetually hungry, and they would consume anything which moved within the range of their rapacious jaws.

Lesser worm-like creatures hungrily devoured any rotting branch which fell, returning the goodness it contained to the roots of the forest as the worms themselves succumbed to the inevitable or were eaten by something else.

The occasional volcanic eruption, sending its mineral rich clouds of dust high into the air, added to the general nutritional level of the earth as the rains brought it down again to feed the ever growing forest and the vast multitude of creatures it contained.

Although there were many radiation hot spots which would last for a very long time indeed, most of the short life elements had lost their gene altering properties, and life stabilized to a degree, with only the odd mutation turning up every now and again to fill a little gap in the now rich panoply of life which was so abundant on earth.

If any humans had survived, they certainly wouldn't have recognized the new earth with its solid green land mantle, complete with the most ferocious collection of carnivorous creatures ever imagined.

✳✳✳

She was tall and well built, with silky jet black hair framing her amber toned face, from out of which shone eyes of deepest clear blue.

As a mother, there was no equal. The twins were her very reason for living, for her very existence.

Not that she over indulged them, she was strict where it was necessary, but they had the best of everything obtainable for their well-being.

Their education far outstripped that of their young friends, such was their ability to learn, and many a time her mate had teased her

160

about this, suggesting that they already knew everything, and were only playing at being schooled.

She didn't really understand why the twins were of such interest to the science faculty, but she tolerated their visits as best she could.

Although they were not always together, what one learnt, the other seemed to know instinctively, and that caused a few raised eyebrows in certain circles.

'You know, I sometimes think you two are just one person' she said jokingly one day, and the twins glanced at each other, simultaneously winked, and the thought flashed between them,

'If she did but know!'

On a shelf in the main room, there rested a deep purple crystal, a thing of great beauty, but no one really knew why it was there, it just was, and always had been, ever since the twins were born.

When all had retired for the night, and the house was still, it sent its singing message across the galaxy to those who needed to know of the progress of nature's latest creation(s).

The End